PENGUIN BOOK

OTHER LULU

Philip Hensher was born in London, where he now lives. He was educated in Yorkshire and at Oxford and Cambridge. He writes regularly for the *Guardian* and the *Spectator*.

Other Lulus is his first novel.

Other Lulus

Philip Hensher

PENGUIN BOOKS

For Maurizio Caserta

PENGUIN BOOKS

Published by the Penguin Group
Penguin Books Ltd, 27 Wrights Lane, London W8 5TZ, England
Penguin Books USA Inc., 375 Hudson Street, New York, New York 10014, USA
Penguin Books Australia Ltd, Ringwood, Victoria, Australia
Penguin Books Canada Ltd, 10 Alcorn Avenue, Toronto, Ontario, Canada M4V 3B2
Penguin Books (NZ) Ltd, 182–190 Wairau Road, Auckland 10, New Zealand

Penguin Books Ltd, Registered Offices: Harmondsworth, Middlesex, England

First published by Hamish Hamilton 1994
Published in Penguin Books 1995
1 3 5 7 9 10 8 6 4 2

Printed in England by Clays Ltd, St Ives plc

ONE

So I stopped spending so much time with my mother. To tell the truth, this was because she went away for six months, and, as I was twelve years old, I went to stay with my grandmother. 'Friederike,' my grandmother said to me in the hall of her house, holding my suitcase, 'your mother has left you here with us. But we'll make the best of it.' In the dark hall of her house, I nodded, believing it.

My grandmother wanted to be intimidating and she wanted to be conventional in about the same degree. But in this six months she tried hard to be nice to me, and do things which would be good for me and which I should enjoy. Every Sunday we went to the art gallery in Berlin, where she lived, where we lived, and looked at paintings. It was something she liked doing, and so we did it.

Now, my grandmother was stout as anything, and when she took me out for a walk or a visit she always took a kind of stick that she called a shooting stick. She'd bought it in England years before. It was to stop her forever having to look around for somewhere to sit down and rest. It folded up and unfolded out abruptly, and had a spike at one end and a flimsy seat at the other. She would often unfold it in the middle of the street, and sit on it while I waited, and strangers, walking around her, looked strangely at her.

She always brought her stick to the gallery, and when she stopped in front of a portrait or a landscape, she would open it up and sit down heavily, wiggling expansively until she'd drilled a small hole in the wood or stone or even marble floor, if it was a bit cracked. That's what I remember. No one in the Berlin gallery minded, I think. She'd been doing it for fifteen or thirty or forty-three years, and in front of each of her favourite paintings there was a small but permanent hole in the floor. My grandmother now lives in England, but you could recreate her tastes from these drillings, if they haven't done the gallery up and filled all the holes.

On these trips, which I disliked very much, she spent all the time talking in a terrifying way, usually about old friends of hers, all of whom she detested, or about people walking by. All this was carried on in a forceful and carrying whisper which made people turn and stare. Until they heard exactly what she was saying, when they would turn back again. But what made her angrier than anything was having to go out with me, and the thought of how badly I was responding to her kindness. She used to ask me, in front of a painting, if I liked it. At first I would say yes, out of politeness. You always say how much you like food other people give you, even if you don't, so I always liked pictures other people showed me.

Sometimes she would tell me about her life. 'Did I ever tell you how I met your grandfather?' she would say, without waiting for an answer. I never told her about my life, and my grandfather never told me about his; but my grandmother had three or four stories – how my mother nearly drowned when she was six, how my grandmother curtsied to the Kaiser, and how she came to marry my grandfather – which she told me until I could recite them.

My grandmother's best friend Frau Egon, the politest woman I ever knew, often came with us on these trips. My mother says 'Thanks', and I say 'Thank you', and my grandmother, if she says anything, says 'Thank you very much'. But only Frau Egon says 'Thank you very much indeed'. And if I liked a painting she showed me, she would beam, and that would be enough for her. My grandmother, on the other hand, thought Frau Egon a great idiot, and if

I said that I liked a painting that either of them liked, how she would be cross. She said straight away that I had no grounds for liking such a thing. I don't know what she meant by 'such a thing'. Usually she liked it herself. The floor in front of the painting was marked with a neat hole. So, after a while, and a few Sunday afternoons, I started to bait her by saying that I didn't know, and then, after a few more Sundays, no, I didn't like it at all. Neither of these seemed to annoy her as much, so, after a week or two, I said how much I liked every painting again. That just depressed her, and after a few completely silent walks round the gallery, my hand and wrist aching with the effort of being held by her tight-lipped rage, we stopped going there altogether.

Maybe Frau Egon missed these trips, but neither of us did. My grandmother could never think, or never tried to think, of anything we could do which I might enjoy. We talked, and that, actually, was enough. What we talked about when she liked me again were her looks. I don't mean the way she looked at me. I mean the way she looked. She didn't talk in a conceited or vain way about her looks, and, in fact, she only ever said one thing. She said she looked like Christa Ludwig. For a long time I didn't know who this Christa Ludwig was. I thought it maybe was one of the friends she was normally so rude about, or maybe an old friend of my grandfather's, though he seemed quite happy without any friends at all. Finally I asked her who this Christa Ludwig was, and instead of hitting her forehead with the palm of her hand, and scowling at my stupidity, which was certainly her normal reaction to my ignorance on any subject whatever, she just said 'Ach' fondly, and put on a record of a woman singing.

The voice was definitely singing in German, but I couldn't understand anything of the words. It was singing in what I then considered a very stupid way, with big swoops and wobbles. It wasn't that you couldn't tell what the words were, though you couldn't. It was that you couldn't tell what the notes were supposed to be. I don't know what she was singing, and I can't remember now what my grandmother's records are like. She strongly objects to coloured sleeves for records, and always covers hers between squares of cardboard. On each makeshift cover there was a code abbreviation – Schub Wint KF 1954 – so you had to fish it out before you could see what it was. This made the record almost worthless, as not even my grandmother could always understand the code. (I suppose it's quite likely that it wasn't Christa Ludwig at all she played to me that day.) This was why she did it, since she always believed that we were going to sell everything of hers as soon as she died. She may have been right.

In any case, she couldn't find a picture of Christa Ludwig. I had only her voice to go on, if it was her voice, and that wasn't any use. Though my grandmother swooped and wobbled quite a bit herself, in church at Christmas and so on, it seemed to me quite a different sort of wobble. So I illogically didn't really believe her. The point of my grandmother's saying she looked like Christa Ludwig, which she did very often, is that after she said it, she would put on a record of Christa Ludwig. And, after a few times, I got to know the songs fairly well, and discovered that you could after all tell what the notes were, though, it's true, not the words. And, after I knew the songs in a sort-of way, I would sing them round the house. One day my grandmother heard me, and I could hear her stop what she was doing, which was complaining to the maid, and I carried on singing. She came into the sitting room, where I was looking out of the window, and said, '*Wie schön! Wie schön!*' And that's how I come to be where I am now, I'm afraid.

Days later, she meant me to hear what she said to my grandfather. She said, 'I heard Friederike singing last week.

And, do you know? It may be that I look like Christa Ludwig. But she will be a new Christa Ludwig.' I knew she meant me to hear this, because she never spoke to my grandfather if she could help it, and certainly never at such length. Even he must have been surprised. He grunted.

When my mother came back from abroad – 'Did you have a nice time?' I said. 'Oh yes,' she said – I told her about her mother looking like Christa Ludwig, and she said, 'Yes, she does.' She went to the shelf in the sitting room in our flat, and got down a box of records, and showed me Christa Ludwig. And Christa Ludwig certainly did look like my grandmother, with a helmet of hard blonde hair and low solemn brow. Of course, I didn't say anything about my being the new Christa Ludwig. I still didn't like the way she sang, though I listened to almost a whole opera to imagine my grandmother taking part in it. 'Why are you listening to that?' said my mother, and I told her. We giggled a little together. I *was* glad to be home.

I got to know my grandmother much better later on, unfortunately, but that's mainly what I remember of her from that time. She used to repeat herself a lot, it's true, though all I remember her *ever* saying is 'She will be the new Christa Ludwig' and '*Wie schön*' and, I suppose, the other things, when she wasn't so pleased with me. But when you're young, it doesn't seem so strange if people say the same things a lot. Perhaps you only think you understand what they mean, and you're pleased if they say it until you really do. Perhaps you like people's characters to be simple enough, even if it means they aren't allowed to say much. In any case, all I remember thinking was not how embarrassing that she repeated herself, but only dislike for her when she praised me.

It was in her drawing room that I started singing properly, with my silent grandfather playing the piano. He would nod to show he was starting, I would join in, and my grandmother would sway, or even, for particular songs (we steered clear of *Die Forelle*) sing quaveringly along. At the end, my grandfather would nod again, not because he was pleased, though he might have been, but just to show it was over. Then there would be the ghost of a smile, his lips pursed like a dowager's. My grandmother would breathe out as if exhaling was new to her, and say, '*Wie schön! Wie schön!*' Sometimes she was just saying this to me, or to me and her maid, Mathilde, but after a while I found she was saying it to an audience of her friends, some of whom said sometimes that they enjoyed it. Some of them, as time went on, even joined in with the swaying.

I never knew, though, who they were saying '*Wie schön*' to. They weren't saying it to me, certainly not. I might have been meant to overhear what they were saying, but that was all. When I was old enough to go to the opera with her, she would sometimes say to me '*Wie schön*' in exactly the same way when the soprano left the stage, although not 'She will be the new Christa Ludwig'. Sometimes it *was* Christa Ludwig. It wouldn't have been polite. Eventually I realized that it wasn't for the singer's benefit, but for the audience's. I wondered from time to time what my grandmother got from saying '*Wie schön*' when the music finished. I never wanted to say anything. I felt more like my grandfather, who would just let the music end, and then nod, with the ghost of a smile, as I said.

Perhaps the question for my grandmother would have been, not what she got out of it, but what the music got out of her, if that makes sense. Perhaps she wanted to join in, to show (but who to?) that she liked something. Because, however strongly you like something, you're not really adding to it by just liking it. If you can sing it, or play it, or read it out loud, I suppose, you're making it yours, and adding something to it. But if you just like it, well, however much, however intensely you like it, you can't change anything. You can leave a mark, or make a noise. And then you're showing other people who like it that you've been there too, that you like it in the same or a different, better way. But they'll probably ignore your mark, or your noise, trying to make their own marks or noises, or, alternatively, creating their own silences and applauses around it.

After my mother came back from abroad, I still went round to my grandmother's house. I went whenever she asked, and usually sang, because it was easier to do that than talk to her and annoy her. It was much better, I must say, visiting her than living with her. After a while I stopped just singing there, and, on my mother's suggestion, I went to a teacher. At first he was deeply shocked, and shook his head, and said how terrible I was. But he could cure all the bad habits I had fallen into for twenty-five marks an hour, and after he had been teaching me for a while, he actually started praising me. So I got another teacher, and he too was deeply shocked, and shook his head, and then, after a year or two, would occasionally say, 'Well, that's not too bad, after all.'

Both these teachers used to say extraordinary things to persuade me to produce sounds more worth listening to. I can't remember all of them, now that Archy has obliterated every other singing teacher I ever had in my mind. One, I remember, used to say that I was tensing all the wrong things, and that I should let my jaw swing like a big bag with three plums in it. I didn't find this very helpful, and I suppose he hadn't made it up but had been told it, as he couldn't explain what he meant. But I tried to think of it anyway. It was that one or the other who said that I should think that my diaphragm was a tiny coal miner, working so hard that the rest of me could relax completely. But it was definitely the other teacher who said the third thing I remember. He used to say that sound should be like a strand of endless spaghetti I was pulling, not, thankfully, from my mouth, but from my forehead. I suppose I was getting better at it all this time, though it seemed as if I was just getting more to worry about, what with the spaghetti and the plums and the coal miners in my belly.

All this time, I was still going back and singing for my grandmother, and the ladies were still mostly putting up with it as if I were as bad as ever. And still she and her polite friend Frau Egon were chorusing 'Ach, the new Christa Ludwig' and '*Wie schön*' and agreeing with each other. My grandfather was there, too, playing the piano and accompanying me, the beloved.

Then he died. And when he died, we found ourselves, four women, like the end of *Buddenbrooks*, trying to think of a time when he lost his temper, and no one could think of one. 'He was so good,' my grandmother had said. 'Did he ever lose his temper?' she said rhetorically. His wife and his wife's best friend for moral support and my mother, his daughter, sat for some time before I remembered a time I knew no one else would remember, or want to remember. Of course I didn't mention it. He was good, but it would have surprised and even shocked my grandmother to have a story like that told about him at his funeral. I suppose she only wanted us to try and think of a time when he lost his temper so that we couldn't.

There was one time, though. And I remembered it, eating the sliced cold meats fanned out by the caterer and Frau Egon after the priest had gone. This was it. Once I arrived early, when some friends of hers were supposed to be coming round, and I was supposed to be singing. The maid, Mathilde, a long-serving disagreeable silent dwarf in black, let me in. I thought no one was in the flat, so, a little nervous of my grandparents and the silent stunted maid, I sat down in the hall. Then, in the drawing room, someone started to play the piano. Now, usually, there was only Chopin or Schubert played in that house, on that piano.

But this was like a violent crash, three vases and a paperweight falling on different parts of the keyboard almost simultaneously. Except that it was immediately repeated, exactly the same, and again, and again, slightly changed, and then again. It was my grandfather.

I listened for a while. I didn't really know what to do. It seemed rude to go in, but I knew my grandmother would be cross if I stayed where I was. I was still standing in the hall, holding my music with both hands, when I heard my grandmother's voice. She shouted something she very often shouted, which was, '*Was machst du denn für Unsinn, du Scheisskerl?*' And the use of the word *Scheisskerl*, which she used for almost everyone she knew, from my mother, an occasional *Scheisskerl*, to the neighbour's dog, a *Scheisskerl* so unvarying I thought for a time that was its name, made me relax. It seemed shocking to most people that an old lady should use such a word in front of a girl, indeed, quite often, about a girl, and it was one of the things which made them enjoyably turn away in art galleries. To me it only meant that my grandmother, though displeased, wasn't seriously displeased, or only ordinarily displeased, and nothing to worry about.

The music, the odd repetitious spasm of notes, abruptly stopped. There was a long silence. I tried to push myself as far into the shadows in the hall as I possibly could. When my grandfather burst out, I was so concerned at not being seen by him that I wouldn't have understood what he was saying if he hadn't said it over and over again. He was shouting '*Scheiss macht frei! Scheiss macht frei!*' I don't know what he meant by that, but, as you see, I couldn't have told the story at his funeral. I was certain he hadn't seen me until he stopped in his unprecedented, cartoon-like, unforgettable rage and shouted, still so loud you could hardly understand him, 'And the girl is here now, what's more.' I liked him for saying 'what's more'. It wasn't as if they were having a discussion, but it made him sound as reasonable as he usually was. Then he went back into the drawing room, shutting the door with alarming care, and afterwards he was the same as he always had been before.

'Stupid,' said my grandmother with surprising tenderness. I hadn't seen her come out of the kitchen, and there she was. What I remember, as if I were watching it in a film, is my own white scared face in the brown shadows of the hallway.

Before my grandfather died, then, there were holes in front of pictures, and Christa Ludwig, and my grandmother quavering along to *Die Forelle*, and the bag of plums, and, I'm afraid, *Scheiss macht frei*. And after he died, Archy changed everything.

TWO

The first thing I noticed about Archy was how often he said sorry. And the second thing was that he never ever looked directly at you.

When I say he said sorry, I don't mean he apologized the whole time, and I don't mean he said *Es tut mir leid*, which everyone says. He would say *Entschuldigung*. This was his only concession to politeness, and it wasn't enough. When I first went to his room, in the conservatory in Vienna, to have a singing lesson, I knocked nervously. There was no reply. I knocked again. There was again no reply. I was thinking of going away when suddenly the door was pulled open. Archy stood there, holding the door with one hand, the frame with the other, very cross, very rumpled, very mad.

'Who are you, anyway?' he said, unreasonably.

I never, as a rule, knew whether to say 'Friederike, Friederike Weissmann', which would be friendly, or the more formal 'Weissmann, Friederike Weissmann'. But this so unnerved me that I said 'Friederike' and left it at that.

'Ah,' said Archy, and, leaving the door open, went back to his desk. I stood at the door for a moment, not sure whether to go in or not. Archy continued to write for a while, and then picked up the telephone and dialled a long number. There was a pause, and then he began to speak in English. I didn't speak English, but I could hear that most of what he was saying was Yes or No. All this time he had his back to me. Finally he said, very firmly and slowly, 'No. No. No,' and dropped the phone on to the cradle, as if it were hot.

'All right, sing,' he said, turning round. 'Well, come in, first, you idiot.'

I went in, dropping papers as I went. I did my best to retrieve them without stopping. Archy watched me for a while, and then said 'Sorry,' without, however, coming to help me. I don't know why he said that, but it made me feel a little better. I stopped, gathered the papers together without fumbling too much. I handed him the piano part of a Mozart aria.

'This is "Martern aller Arten",' I said. It was something I used to sing a lot, since it was very hard.

'I can see that,' said Archy, looking at the piano part. 'How appropriate. Tortures of every kind. No, I don't want to hear this, thank you very much.'

I surprised myself by saying, 'Why not?'

'Because I don't care for it, and I don't think you can sing it,' he said. 'Sorry.'

'Why not?' I said again.

'Because nobody can sing it, of course,' he said. 'Sing something else.'

'I can't think of anything else,' I said. 'Sorry.'

'All right,' said Archy. 'Here's something else.'

He handed something over. It said at the top, 'Photocopying Strictly Forbidden'. It was a photocopy. I could see immediately that I couldn't sing it. It was what old old ladies used to call 'modern music', putting the emphasis scornfully on the second syllable of 'modern'. It was full of leaps and bounds and sevenths and ninths, and empty of anything resembling a scale. My scales were famous in the Grünewald, and I wanted to show them off.

Archy played some notes on the piano. I became very angry and cold. I looked at the knots of notes and began to sing very seriously. I thought about my diaphragm, working away like a tiny coal miner in my belly, I thought about the stream of sound I was about to pull like a strand of spaghetti from my head, and I sang two notes. Archy stopped me.

'Wrong note,' he said. 'Or, rather, notes. Sorry.'

He played the first five notes very slowly. I nodded.

'No,' he said. 'Sing them, you fool.'

I tried, and tried again. He played them at the right speed, and then, impatiently, very fast. I tried again.

'All right,' he said. He started to play the piano part. I started to sing, blushing with rage at his unfairness. He let me carry on. I knew I was wrong, but I didn't stop. I could feel from the way the piano was shaking on its casters that he was laughing violently and silently. In the end I made a very ugly noise and then, consumed with fury, I burst into the very difficult long fast scale that comes halfway through 'Martern aller Arten'. Archy stopped playing and looked at me for the first time.

'You're terrible,' he said eventually. 'Go away. Take this with you. Come back when you can sing. Not when you can sing this. When you can sing. I suppose I'm to teach you all year this year. Sorry.'

I took the music from him, trying not to snatch, and concentrated hard on not crying before I got out.

'One more thing,' he said as I put my hand on the door. 'While you're teaching yourself to sing, don't listen to anyone else singing. Listen to someone who can play the viola really well.'

'What do you mean?' I said, although I still meant to leave.

'Do you shoot?' he said.

'No,' I said. 'Why, do you?'

'I thought Germans, or rather Austrians,' he said, 'thought every Englishman could shoot.'

'I'm German,' I said. 'I didn't know that.'

'Well, they do,' he said, waiting for me to go. I was fairly sure I wasn't going to cry now, so I turned and sat down.

'Germans or English?' I said.

'German or English what?' he said.

'Do all Germans believe that all Englishmen shoot, or,' I said, losing the track of what I was saying, 'do all Englishmen believe that too?'

'Sorry,' said Archy. 'But look. If you're shooting, you don't look at what you're aiming at. You aim at something else, and then you'll hit it.'

'But if you aim at something completely different then you won't,' I said.

'Oh,' he said. 'If you can't see what I'm saying you oughtn't to listen.'

Then he turned round to the piano and started to play a Chopin waltz incredibly badly. It reminded me of my grandfather, who used to play such things, though rather better, and it was still reminding me when Archy stopped and, without turning round, said, 'Go away, please.'

I went.

I think now what he was trying to do was to scare me so much that I would fall slightly in love with him. In the books I read, women were always meeting men who seemed bad but were really good, but falling in the first place for men who seemed good but weren't. They usually found out the error of their ways, unfortunately. I used to think that a man who seemed good to everyone else but was actually rather wicked and bad would suit me quite well. Archy was a great reader, and I suppose he thought that it would save time if he seemed bad all along. There might be women who would reach the conclusion that anyone who seemed so rude and bad must be a true and a good person, though it seemed improbable.

Anyway, I went along the next week.

'You again,' he said.

'Yes, of course,' I said. 'This is my time, isn't it?'

'Can you sing now?' he said.

I looked around at his room. It was strangely tidy, with books neatly lined up rather than in piles on the floor, like most people's. The books were all gold-embossed, cheap novels five centimetres thick and with titles one word long. There were bottles of whisky and gin on a table. No one else at the school had bottles in his room like that.

'Of course,' I said. 'Shall we start with the Weber?'

'Webern, you idiot,' he said. 'Sorry. Let's go.'

He played a few notes. I joined in. I sang to the end. I noticed all the mistakes he made, but he didn't put me off. I thought about coal miners, and bags of fruit, and spaghetti, and made beautiful noises in the right place and at the right time. We reached the end, which just stopped rather than finished properly.

'My god,' Archy said. 'You're terrible. Absolutely terrible. But you can stay this week.'

'I don't like it,' I said.

'What?' he said.

'The song, of course,' I said.

'Why not?' he said.

'It doesn't end,' I said. 'Not properly.'

'Of course it doesn't,' he said. 'It's not meant to. It's the second song in a set of three.'

'How does the third one end?' I said.

'Much the same way,' he said.

'Well, then,' I said. 'And it's really unmemorable. I mean, it doesn't stay in your mind.'

'Sorry,' he said. 'But it doesn't need you to remember it to be memorable. You're just a singer.'

'Anyway,' I said. 'I managed to remember it.'

'Most of it,' Archy said.

THREE

This was in Vienna. When my grandfather died, he left me all his money, and it turned out to be an enormous amount. In that odd period between his funeral and the reading of his will, I visited my grandmother. She was out, but Mathilde, her dwarfish maid, was in. She was dressed in black, but then she always was. I liked her fastidious lack of friendliness, and I went and sat with her in the kitchen.

'Don't do that, please,' she said.

'I'm not doing anything,' I said. I was looking through the refrigerator for something to eat.

'There isn't anything,' she said. 'I could make you some coffee, I suppose, if you want to wait for your grandmother.'

I didn't particularly, but I said Yes, and Mathilde went about it with no noticeable enthusiasm.

'You know,' I said, 'when I go and see anybody else, and go and sit in their kitchens, there's always a new sort of Viennese coffee cake to try. Or anyway an old sort of Viennese coffee cake to eat.'

'Don't be ridiculous,' Mathilde said. 'There only is one sort of Viennese coffee cake. What you mean is, you saw it on the television. Well, I've got better things to do with my time.'

'Like what?' I said.

'None of your business,' she said.

Conversation lapsed for a while.

'Do you miss my grandfather?' I said.

'In a certain way,' she said. 'Yes, I do.'

'Less laundry, I suppose,' I said.

'No,' she said fiercely. 'No. I miss him. No one plays the piano any more.'

'Where did my grandfather's money come from?' I said, not really wanting to get into this. I had never really been able to ask this, and since neither my grandmother nor my mother were particularly keen to talk about money, I never knew it.

'Here and there,' Mathilde said. 'Not that it's any of my business. Not that it's any of your business, either.'

'What do you mean, here and there?' I said.

'He always had it,' Mathilde said. 'Shares and so on. You know he never worked.'

'Yes,' I said.

'Family money,' she said.

I was suspicious of Mathilde's scrupulous vagueness, but in fact when later I came to talk to my grandfather's accountant, I discovered that this was absolutely true. My grandfather's money all came from his family; he had hardly added to it at all, but had always lived on the income from it. Naturally, it was not what it had been, but he had begun with such an enormous sum thirty years before that it turned out to be still a satisfyingly huge amount, and for a while my bank statements thudded on my doormat like sacks of gold.

As I was leaving, since my grandmother never turned up, I said to Mathilde, 'Well, you could always get someone else to play the piano, you know.'

'It wouldn't be the same,' she said scornfully. 'They'd play other people's music.'

'It would be exactly the same,' I said back. 'Anyone can play what my grandfather used to play.'

'They wouldn't play the music he used to play,' she said. 'They wouldn't play his music, would they?'

'His music?'

'Music he wrote,' she said. 'You didn't know he wrote

music, did you? That's something you didn't know, anyway.'

I left, unable to cope with Mathilde any more. But I really didn't know that my grandfather wrote music at all, and I would have asked my grandmother about it, if the reading of the will hadn't come first. The will, with its terrible and amusing burden, caused my grandmother not only to stop talking to me, but to stop looking at me. Both my mother and I assumed that this was because of grief, and that she wasn't seeing anyone. It seems unlikely now, since he was the most invariable *Scheisskerl* of all, apart from the neighbour's dog. But then I started to meet the sort of ladies who I would sing to at my grandmother's, and I realized it wasn't true.

Once I met Frau Egon in the street. She was my grandmother's best friend. She was smily, charming, sixty-four. We were both moping, though, it's true, in completely different ways, and she asked me about my grandmother.

'I haven't seen her for a long time,' I said.

'No,' she said. 'I was thinking that I hadn't seen you there for a while. We do miss your singing so very much. But of course.'

'Oh yes,' I said, 'of course,' in such a way that Frau Egon realized immediately that she had said something wrong and tottered off in paroxysms of combined embarrassment and fear at what my grandmother would have to say. It didn't altogether surprise me that my grandmother had simply decided to stop seeing me, nor that she was certainly complaining to all her friends about me. I went home, wrote a cheque for a hundred thousand marks to my grandmother to make her feel at least a little guilty. And then I went to Vienna, to study at the conservatory and to play at being a poor student for a while. And for a while it was fun.

*

After my first lesson with Archy I telephoned my mother. She told me that my grandmother had still not asked where I was or what I was doing. However, she knew that I had gone somewhere, since now she would telephone my mother without being asked to. I told her about Archy, and tried to make it sound a little like a funny story. She told me that Vienna was very beautiful at that time of year, or, come to think of it, at any time of year. She always said that. Then she said, 'Anything else?' since she was worried about my telephone bill. This always amused me. I just said, 'I've moved again,' and gave her my new telephone number. She sighed, but then she always did that, too.

The next week I went to Archy's room without the music, having practised so much, to the irritation of my new flatmates, that I didn't need it.

'OK?' said Archy. He was lying face down on his sofa reading a brick of a novel, open on the floor.

'OK,' I said, waiting for him to get up or at least stop reading.

'You can play the piano for yourself this week,' he said, when it became apparent that I was waiting for him. 'I'm too bored.'

'I can't,' I said.

'What,' he said, 'can't play the piano?'

'No,' I said. 'And, anyway, I haven't got the music.'

'Well, go and get it,' he said.

'I don't need it,' I said. 'I can remember it.'

Archy got up slowly and went to the drinks table, letting the book fan itself shut. He poured himself a drink, either gin or vodka, I couldn't see which. He added some tonic water. It was English tonic water, which in Vienna is very expensive. I suppose that was why he didn't use a great deal of it.

'You can remember it?' he said. 'I don't believe it. In the first place you can't have. In the second I'm not interested in learning things off by heart. I'm only interested in the music, and the music means the piece of paper and the ink, and only then the sounds you happen to feel like making on that particular day. I don't believe you'll ever impress anyone by singing Webern off by heart inaccurately. Either they'll know the song and see that you're getting it wrong, or they won't and think that you're making it up. So what,' he said, taking a gulp, 'is the fucking point?'

'The point is,' I said, 'that I *can* remember it.' I would have put a fucking in, but I found it hard to work out where it should go.

'Well done. Ten out of ten. Off by heart,' said Archy, and the phrase 'off by heart' suddenly had such resonances of irony it was as if they had always been there. 'All right. Off we go.'

He sat down at the piano and began to play. He didn't bother to take the music down. I started to sing. I could hear that he was playing something else, or making something up that wasn't the song. I carried on. I finished. He played a little trill, then stopped. I noticed that one side of his face was quite red from where he had been lying on the sofa.

'Sorry. I don't think that was quite accurate, Friederike,' he said.

'No,' I said.

'You see,' he said. 'Were you making it up, or was I? How do we tell? Neither of us has the music. It sounded all right to me.'

'That's because you were making it up,' I said.

'True,' he said.

FOUR

'Are you English?' I said to Archy one day, at random.

'Mm-hmm,' he said back, unhelpfully. It was an English noise, but I didn't know what it meant; I didn't know at all.

That summer I moved so many times in my attempt to be a poor student in defiance of my bank balance that I hardly bothered to unpack my suitcases. Nobody I knew could understand why I didn't simply buy a flat. Neither could I, really. But I moved so many times that I became expert in assembling my record player, which at first had seemed such an impossible task. I would lug things up stairs, and half an hour later the owner of the flat would sit and watch me attaching one wire to another and plugging plugs into sockets with such confidence that later they would always ask me mend their bicycles, or unblock sinks, expectation bright on their faces. I always refused. There was no point. I knew I wouldn't stay long enough to do the task twice.

Three weeks later, I would find myself unplugging the record player and disassembling the fold-up waist-high bookcase and negotiating with unwilling taxi drivers – on two occasions the same taxi driver. I never stopped reading the columns of the Viennese papers, never stopped arriving at the newspapers' offices at six on the day of publication. My card was a permanent fixture on the notice-board of the conservatory. 'Student of singing, 21, seeks room in flat, central, cheap, no cats, no non-smokers, no vegetarians, no Lesbians.' It didn't say that. It should have. I lived with a succession of cat-owning non-smoking vegetarian Lesbians in the expensive outer suburbs of Vienna. At most I stayed six weeks, at least, ten minutes. It was oddly enjoyable.

'Where did you see my notice?' said a girl as I sat in her kitchen, drinking very horrible coffee with my coat still on.

'At the conservatory,' I said.

'At the where?' she said.

'I study singing,' I said.

'Oh, of course,' she said. 'I have a very dear friend at the conservatory. He must have. He very kindly put it up there for me.'

'Oh right,' I said. 'I assumed you were a music student. I just thought you must be.'

'Alas, no,' she said, smiling in a way which made me think she didn't do it very often. 'But my friend.'

'Right,' I said. Everyone I ever met knew someone who was at the conservatory, or who was a very good singer, or who was very fond of Schumann's *Lieder*. I didn't care to follow it up.

'The rent is payable on the first of the month,' she said. 'Bills extra.'

It was the tenth, and I didn't think I would be staying until the first. There were five rooms in the flat. One was a bedroom which she slept in. One was a bedroom I slept in. One was a kitchen. One was a bathroom. One was a room for everything else. All the rooms were painted white, with cheap flowered curtains at the windows, and on the walls, instead of pictures, were reproductions of famous paintings, too small really to look at. All the furniture was covered in the same flowered materials as the curtains. Every room was tidy, because there was nothing in it except furniture and what she called her ornaments. There were no saucepans big enough to cook anything in, and there were no knives sharp enough to slice anything with, but there was a device to press garlic into a paste, which the girl once seriously recommended to me, when she saw me chopping a piece of garlic with a knife, as an invaluable tool. The only money she ever seemed to spend on herself was on bath oils, and shampoos, and hair oils, and skin preparations, and for one evening in three she sat around, her face and hair covered in various forms of lard in various alarming colours, flicking through magazines she bought and read and then threw away directly.

She kept her house without heat, and allowed me to warm the water for a bath for an hour every other day. If I complained about the cold, she pointed out that I was only wearing a shirt, and that I should dress more warmly. She habitually wore an overcoat around the flat, eating her breakfast in the bare kitchen, standing, dressed for the street. This gave her an air of rushed purposiveness, when she should only have seemed mean. I sang continuously and hugged myself, when alone, to keep warm. Her name was Charlotte and I detested her. Bills were extra, but there weren't really any to speak of, except the telephone, and I don't think I ever paid that.

One day Archy told me to sing 'Martern aller Arten'. I stood with my feet apart and my hands behind my back and practised breathing during the very long introduction. Just as Archy reached the point where I came in, he stopped and apologized for his mistakes, and started again. He played the piano with flamboyant badness. I sang it all the way through, resting my hand on the piano top like a diva.

'That was terrible,' Archy said. 'What were you thinking about?'

'What were *you* thinking about?' I asked, stung.

'I was thinking how terrible you are,' he said. 'What were you thinking about?'

'I was thinking about the genius of Mozart,' I said.

'It was a serious question, you know,' he said.

'Well,' I said. 'I was concentrating on relaxing my jaw

and working hard with my diaphragm and producing an unbroken stream of sound.' I didn't like to tell him the silly metaphors I used, in case he thought I had made them up myself. Nor did I want to tell him about the rubbish that usually filled my mind when I sang.

'Mm-hmm,' he said. 'Sorry, but do you have any stories you use about your diaphragm and your jaw, or anything?'

'Stories?'

'Like, your jaw is made of jelly and your diaphragm is made of iron and your throat isn't really there at all?'

'Like –?'

'Like whatever. Stop it.'

'It helps me, though.'

'It doesn't help.'

He came up to me and put his hand on my stomach.

'Think whatever you think when you sing,' said Archy, 'and then sing something.'

I sang a burst of Mozart to plums and coal miners and spaghetti.

'Now think of Charlotte,' said Archy. 'No, don't say anything, just sing.'

I did a burst of Webern to Charlotte in her overcoat in the cold flat. Archy's hand was on my stomach the whole time, palpitating.

'You see?' said Archy.

I didn't. I sang again, thinking first of nothing, and then concentrating on Archy's hand, which he hadn't taken from my stomach, squeezing my stomach like dough.

'You see now?' said Archy.

'No,' I said. 'How do you know Charlotte?'

'Oh, the usual way,' he said. 'I don't imagine you get on very well.'

'The very dear friend,' I murmured.

'What?' Archy said.

'We don't, actually,' I said.

'No. But look. Did you feel any different when you were thinking about whatever you think about to how you felt when you weren't thinking about anything?'

'I think about my jaw feeling loose as a bag of plums,' I said, 'and my diaphragm working as hard as a coal miner.' I said this because I had to say something. Archy's very dear friendship with Charlotte had come into the room, and made me blush at his hand still massaging my stomach.

'Your diaphragm,' Archy said. 'Hm. Your diaphragm should be working as hard as a tin miner, not as a coal miner.' He took his hand away, and I realized that he had actually forgotten that he had his hand on my stomach until I had reminded him by mentioning my diaphragm.

'How hard does a tin miner work?' I said.

'Oh, very, very hard,' said Archy. He turned round to the table behind him, and took the bottle of gin. He poured a glass and topped it with tonic water. Then he took a small bottle, like the bottles my grandmother kept filled with oil to pour in her ears. The label was stained almost black with ancient spillages. He unscrewed the top with a crusty whisper of deposit falling from the rim, and, raising the glass and the bottle unnecessarily to the light, knocked the bottle two or three times against the lip of the glass, clouded the glass with pink. 'Yum yum,' he said. It was another English noise, although a less ambiguous one.

FIVE

I asked Charlotte about Archy and this is what she told me.

Archy was the son of a Lord and came from England. He was a very great singer who had performed at Covent Garden, which was an opera house in England, but had decided to give up his career in opera to teach in Vienna. Despite frequent telephone calls from the great opera houses of Milan and New York and San Francisco and Paris and Berlin and Rome, all offering him contracts to sing whatever he wished at whatever figure he cared to name, he gave the whole thing up to create singers greater even than himself. I think Charlotte got this bit slightly wrong, as I had been to the opera in Rome and it was not a great opera house, but a theatre filled with ladies in furs singing along to Bulgarian sopranos in *Madame Butterfly*. Gradually the telephone calls dried up, but Archy's life was complete. He took the occasional pupil which his job insisted on. He was enormously rich and learned and cultivated and pursued by not only opera houses but duchesses of every description.

Then Charlotte told me how she knew Archy. She told me that she had studied English at university many years before, and that to perfect her English she had gone to England. There she had met Archy's family. She had stayed many times with Lord Harcourt in his great castle, or palace, or, as Charlotte put it – she liked to drop English words and phrases into her fastidiously subjunctived German – his *stately home*. She hinted until I could no longer pretend to be obtuse that she and Archy had had an affair. He had come to Vienna principally to pursue his genius, but also so that she and he could be together. However, she had decided that his work could benefit the world so much that she could not justify distracting him from it. They therefore no longer saw each other.

What I thought of Archy was . . . But that can wait. This glittering tosh of Charlotte's, which she told so slowly, in hints and suggestions, until my jaw ached with encouragement and smiling and saying, 'But I don't quite understand . . .' convinced me not a jot. I did not believe that he was the son of a Lord, nor that he was enormously rich. *I* was enormously rich; I could spot the type. Nor that he was particularly cultivated, nor that he could sing at all. He had never sung when I was around, and, in my experience, anyway, most people who could sing could hardly resist an invitation to sing, were forever trilling and warbling to elicit praise for the smoothness of the transition between their registers, or whatever.

What I did believe was that Archy and Charlotte had had an affair.

Once I was sitting in Charlotte's kitchen with her, and I was boiling some water on the stove, supposedly so that I could eventually put some potatoes into it, but in fact so that it would warm the kitchen. We were both wearing overcoats. Charlotte was telling me about an evening she had spent with Archy at a performance of *Tristan*, and Archy had wept with grief as he would never now sing the part of Tristan. I knew this was nonsense as she had previously told me that he was a baritone. She was telling me this when the telephone rang.

'Hello!' she said. 'Hello! Well! Hello!'

Then she was silent for a moment.

'One second, please,' she said, and handed me the receiver.

'Hello, Archy,' I said, maliciously, before he said anything.

He was calling, very surprisingly, to ask if I would go out for dinner with him. I had assumed that he wouldn't want to spend any time with me. He never offered me a drink during the lessons, though he habitually drank while teaching. He never prolonged a lesson beyond an hour and often cut it rather short. He always ignored me in the corridors of the conservatory, keenly observing the ground as he walked. I thought that the only contact I was going to have with him outside the lessons, which were made up mostly of insults, would be saying hello to the top of his head.

Intrigued, I accepted. 'You'll have to pay for yourself, you know,' he said.

'That's all right,' I said.

'Oh well then,' he said.

'Do you want to talk to Charlotte?' I said. She was still in the room.

'Christ, no,' he said. 'Six-thirty tonight. Come to my office.'

Archy, like Charlotte, was wearing his overcoat in his office when I arrived. I thought he must just have come in, but in fact he was just going out. I wondered if he would have waited for me if I hadn't arrived just then, so little did he appear to notice me. We walked downstairs without speaking. I wanted to wait until he spoke, but he defeated me with his demanding silence and his head-down walk.

'How well do you know Charlotte?' I said.

'Quite well,' he said, unsurprised.

'She seems to know you very well,' I said. 'She was pleased you telephoned.'

'Even though I didn't want to talk to her?' asked Archy.

'Not so pleased, I suppose,' I said.

'I suppose so,' he said.

'She says she knows you very well,' I said.

'Yes,' he said, in such a neutrally final tone that I

couldn't tell whether he meant that he knew her very well after all, that he understood and appreciated the suggestion that they had had an affair, or simply that she was the sort of girl who might well think that she knew him even though she really didn't. Which she was.

The bar I went to with Archy was such a very un-Viennese bar that I had no idea that bars like it existed in Vienna. The walls were concrete and polished to a dull shine. The music was loud and the metal tables shook, and the windows were in the ceiling, and you could see the soles of shoes walking over them, since the bar was underground. When I looked in the half-reflecting grey walls, it was easy to see that my round face was very unlike the other faces in the bar, and, taller than almost anyone else in the bar, I was looked at by the obvious regulars.

Archy found a table for us and went off. I held my bag in my lap with both hands. It was a brown bag, a colour nowhere else in that black room. Archy had gone not to the lavatory, as I had thought, but to the bar, perhaps to say hello to someone. The barman looked at him in a strange way as he said something, then poured two beers. Archy was already holding out a note as the barman handed the beers across. The barman looked at it. Then, realizing that Archy meant to pay, he wiped his hands and took the note. He had to walk to the far end of the bar to find any change, and back again to give it to Archy. Archy thoughtfully juggled the coins from one palm to another, took one, whether the smallest or the largest I couldn't see, and dropped it in a saucer on the bar. The barman looked at it, looked at me, looked at Archy and left it there.

'No one ever wants to be paid in Vienna,' said Archy, putting two beers down, which I didn't want and hadn't asked for.

'Yes they do,' I said. 'They just want to be paid at the normal time.'

'What do you mean?' said Archy after a pause. He raised his eyes from the table and looked directly at me. He was suddenly angry, whether with me or not, I don't know, but I wasn't to be daunted and I carried on.

'You don't pay when you get the drink,' I said. 'You pay when you leave. And they come to your table anyway, you don't have to go to the bar,' I added in a rush of correctitude.

'Mm-hmm,' said Archy. He drank. He put his glass down. I picked mine up and drank too quickly. When I had stopped coughing he was looking at me.

'How can you afford to come to Vienna to study?' he said.

'Easily,' I said.

'You haven't got a scholarship from us, have you?'

'No,' I said.

'I thought not,' he said. 'Have you tried gargling with salt and water, incidentally?'

'No,' I said. 'Why?'

'Improves tone production,' he said. 'And you haven't got any kind of official grant, as far as I can see.'

'Or find out,' I said. 'No, I haven't.'

'So?' he said.

'I pay for it myself,' I said.

'It's very expensive,' he said.

'I'm very rich,' I said.

'And is it worth it,' he said, 'all this expensive tuition which you can easily afford?'

'Not so far,' I said.

'Someone would have said something before now,' he said, throwing me slightly until I realized he was still talking about paying for the beer.

'It's true, anyway,' I said.

'I've been in Vienna three years and no one's ever told me that before,' he said.

'Have you always been going to the bar and paying for each drink before you know if there's something wrong with it?' I said.

'Yes,' he said.

'And no one's ever tried to tell you not to before now?'

'No,' he said.

I began to laugh, an odd sound in the concrete bar, odd as my brown kleenex-full bag.

'I don't have many friends in Vienna,' he said.

'I thought not,' I said. 'Only Charlotte. But where were you before?'

'England,' he said, surprised, as if it were the normal place to come from.

'And people pay for their drinks, in England, before they drink them, and they have to go to the bar every time they want another one, which is very often in England I suppose, and by the time they want to complain about it they've paid and they can't?'

'Of course, of course, of course!' said Archy. He was very cross and didn't want to look at me any more, but I didn't mind because I was winning. I knew all that about England, anyway. I wanted to tease him because, although my bag was brown and my laugh and my clothes and even my round face wrong in Archy's modish bar, I felt strong and buoyed up by antagonism.

'And the beer is warm, too. It's delicious, though,' said Archy, a little pathetically, trying again. 'In England.'

'I know all that, actually,' I said. 'In fact you can get perfectly good *bitter* in Vienna. Perhaps even here.'

I had won.

'How do you get on with Charlotte?' he said.

'Not well,' I said.

'No,' he said. 'I can see that. She's quite difficult.'

'No,' I said. 'I don't think she's difficult. I think she's just an awful liar.'

'That's probably true,' said Archy.

'I mean, she says she knows you terribly well,' I said.

'Well, she does,' he said. 'Why shouldn't she?'

'She said you'd had an affair, too,' I said, untruthfully.

'Who said we'd had an affair?'

'Charlotte did,' I said. 'I said she was an awful liar.'

'What else has she told you about me?' said Archy, spilling his beer in concentration.

'That you had an affair, and that you knew each other in England, and that your father's a Lord, and that you gave up an operatic career to teach here, but only because she was here and you were in love with her,' I said. Now I said it, it seemed less improbable, though not less annoying. It was only Charlotte who covered the whole thing with unlikeliness.

'Well,' said Archy, 'some of that's true.'

'What?' I said, bluntly.

'Some of what you said,' he said. 'She dislikes you, I'm sure of it.'

'Oh, I thought so,' I said, not minding.

What I then expected Archy to ask was what everyone always asked if they knew I was rich and disliked my flatmate. People always asked why I didn't buy somewhere to live, but I never knew what to say. So I was a little relieved when Archy didn't ask this, but said instead, 'Why don't you move into my flat?'

'Yes, all right,' I said, producing an answer before my surprise caught up with me.

Archy beamed, and I thought about Vienna. I thought about my mother saying how beautiful it was at that time of year, or, come to think of it, at any time of year. I thought about its gilded domes and spires and its silvery stone. I thought about the white silky sail-like buildings billowing windowed out over every street with grave beauty. I thought about the strange dark faces, lit from below, unsmilingly observing the passage of time, the rise and fall of palaces, mosques, cathedrals and empires from street corners. I thought about the clouds over Vienna, and I said Yes to Archy.

'You can move in as soon as you like,' he said, later. 'It makes no difference to me.'

I never got anything to eat that night, but I nodded when he said this, believing him.

SIX

In the last days of September 1972, the clouds over Vienna divided, enlarged, inflated. Theatrically lit from behind, they didn't move for days, waiting for something. People stopped in the streets, looked upwards and said 'Clouds' to perfect strangers, a vocative to their gravity and stillness. There was nothing else to say, but they demanded comment.

(And stacked like plates over Vienna the aeroplanes circled the busy sky, waiting for earth.)

On the fifth day the clouds began to move, scudding like yachts across the blue, and by the sixth day Vienna was grey again. People stopped commenting, forgot the unmoving clouds showing the earth what light was like.

I remembered that Gainsborough sky, and I knew what the proper comment would have been, but I said nothing, gargling with salt and water twice a day.

SEVEN

I had too much money, and Archy never had enough. He always had difficulty paying the rent, and often the rent I paid Archy was the only rent he paid the landlord. But, though I had too much money, and he hadn't enough, I had no possessions, and he had too many.

It never occurred to me to buy anything. I went along, buying a new pair of shoes every four months, and a new pair of trousers or a skirt every year, and a new winter coat every three years. A book every so often, a record every so often, and occasionally a hat, or a scarf, or something I only liked, and never wore, because I didn't need it. My wardrobe was empty, and half of my clothes were unwearable with age or size, and I never thought about them. All I ever bought was food, and the only things I owned which I worried about were the four sharp knives I chopped food with.

Before I lived with Archy, I thought he was much like me. His clothes were old and rumpled and burnt round the edges and always the same. He had a bookshelf of bad novels, a piano and a table with gin on it in his room, and that was it.

But when I saw his flat, I realized that Archy was someone who could not leave the flat without buying something, and once he had bought something – even a magazine – he could not throw it away. Every shelf was full of the worst books I had ever read, including the shelves in the kitchen (the saucepans on the floor, the plates on the table). Music, papers, records, more books, piled on the sofas in every room, on the piano, on the bed. There were

Persian carpets everywhere, too big for their rooms, on top of each other, crawling up the walls, and paintings, some on the walls, some in stacks on tables, mirrors with gilt flaking cupids and flowers and fruit and cards wedged into the frames, little toys to be broken, drawers full of tablecloths, pointless fun items of stationery, and pointless gadgets – he never cooked – to cook with (tongs to peel the caul from kidneys, probes to take the middle out of pineapples), and nowhere, anywhere in the flat, did I ever find a single object that did not have a pattern or a picture on it.

The flat swallowed me up, me and my three boxes. There was no question that the second bedroom could be cleared of all the stuff in it to make room for my stuff. There were simply too many things. So I had a few little corners, and I threw a few things away. But Archy was the sort of person that drops things, and I was the sort of person that knocks things over. In some ways I made it worse, since although I like to cook, I do not like to do the washing up afterwards, and it rarely occurred to Archy to wash anything other than, sometimes, his clothes. Soon it would have taken a day of hard work to clear the flat, and another day of uncalculated inactivity would have been enough to return it to the state it was in before.

'If you're going to live here,' said Archy before I went back to Berlin to visit my mother, 'you ought to learn how to drink gin.' He was eyeing my attempts to suppress a cough rather balefully. 'So here is a teaching aid.'

He gave me three big bottles of English gin, which I was to take back to Berlin and conscientiously drink my way through in a fortnight, at the end of which I would like English gin and be a fit person to live with, in Archy's view. I took no clothes or suitcase back to Berlin, but just a heavy carrier bag with these bottles. I knew my old clothes would still be at home, waiting for me, enough for two weeks. And if not, I could always buy some more. So on Friday, I put my clothes, my record player, my fifty records, my two pictures, my twenty books, all into boxes ready to move out. They were the same supermarket boxes I had used to move in.

I left Charlotte's cold flat with the white walls and, with no need for taxis, walked to the railway station. As I walked, I sang Webern, quite happily. People looked at me as I walked through the streets, a woman with no coat or hat but a bag with three bottles in it, baying in full operatic style, shrieks and wails intruding on their Viennese lives, and people just smiled or just looked at me.

When I was younger I had a fear of falling asleep in public places. It's a common fear, though also a common experience. You're afraid of snoring if you snore, or dribbling if you dribble, or, if you know you don't do either, you might be afraid of something quite trivial, falling asleep with your mouth open and looking ugly and foolish. Or, if you read children's stories as a child, you might be afraid of having your luggage stolen or your pocket picked or money taken from your wallet and counterfeit money put there instead. I used to worry about practically all these things. But, singing in the street that day was rather like not worrying any more, waking up in a library with your mouth open, dribbling, and your throat sore with the effort of snoring, and people staring at you, and you thinking only how embarrassing it must have been for *them*, the poor things.

On the way to the station, I realized that the worst thing about making a spectacle of yourself is worrying about it. If you simply stopped worrying about singing in public, while there was no telling where you might end up, there was suddenly nothing wrong with it at all. I don't know why I felt like this, but, sloughing an old self like a snake as I walked, this was the reason why I was quite looking forward to seeing my grandmother, who had always realized this.

It didn't cross my mind that my grandmother wouldn't see me. The chance of blame and recrimination would be too delicious to renounce. So after I left the gin at my mother's flat, I got back in the taxi and gave my grandmother's address to the driver. A kind of glee filled me. I didn't know whether my grandmother had cashed the cheque I had left, or had decided that it wasn't my fault but my grandfather's. I was looking forward to tormenting her and I couldn't stop grinning.

When I rang the bell, there was a long wait, and then a surprised crackling pause as I said my name. The door gave its familiar ordinary fart and I pushed it open. In the past my grandmother or Mathilde had often waited with the door open for me. They both shouted much the same things down the stairwell. 'You're late', or 'None of you ever warn me you're coming, do you?' But this time I had to knock. There was a far-away theatrical groan and a faint shuffle. I waited.

'Oh, it's you,' my grandmother said, as if I hadn't announced myself properly. 'I suppose you want to come in.'

Mathilde was standing at the kitchen door, wiping a plate. My grandmother turned laboriously and hobbled off, giving a very good impersonation of an old woman. I followed. I don't know what I was expecting after a few months away – weeks of dust, food rotting, my grandmother twenty years older or dressed in her wedding gown. But, apart from the limp, and I expect Mathilde had seen to that, everything was the same as ever.

'How well you look,' I said, smoothly.

'She's very well indeed,' said Mathilde, coming in, not to bring coffee or cakes, but just to stand at the door wiping the plate and gazing at us.

'Thank you,' my grandmother said. 'There's no reason why I shouldn't. That's all, thank you very much.'

Mathilde shrugged and left. The piano had been closed and a white lace cloth placed over it, like an allegory of silence. On the top of the piano were forty or so photographs of my grandfather, all in silver frames. They had all been taken quite recently, when he was frail and absent. He always knew when a photograph was imminent, and in all of them had rearranged his features into that fixed accusing glare familiar from our photo albums, but not from life, where his characteristic expression was a sweet thoughtfulness, his gaze directed about a foot to the right of your face. I don't suppose he was thoughtful, and he had every right to look accusing. He never looked much like himself in photographs, but these fifty terrifying, almost identical photographs, glaring at my grandmother were – were what? Authentic? Real? True? None of these. They were only pleasing.

I picked one up. It was different from the rest. My grandfather, unmistakable, was younger. He was with a man of some beauty, in a field. The other man was too well dressed for the field, but my grandfather's boots were muddy. In the lucent glow of old monochrome prints, the two of them appeared to have been placed and arranged by art, lit and half-shadowed to bring out the noble lines in one man's face, the sincere frown in my grandfather's. Gazing sideways, deep in thought or perhaps not thinking at all, or perhaps thinking deeply about the photographer's stained tie, or their indigestion, or something else, lost for ever, outside the photograph, they seemed different from me, and they seemed good, which they were not. There was something about the beautiful soft black of their clothes and the beautiful distant glow of the grey sky which made them both seem either very full of thought or very empty. They were difficult faces to like, but I liked to go on looking at them, and when I put the photograph down I had already forgotten that one of them was my grandfather.

'Do you know who that is?' my grandmother said.

'It's my grandfather,' I said.

'The other man,' she said.

'No,' I said. 'Did ordinary people look like that then?'

'Like what? What do you mean?' she said.

'So beautiful,' I said. 'I've never seen anyone so beautifully dressed, it looks like a film still.'

She looked at me strangely, because the beauty of the people in the photograph belonged to the photograph and not to their clothes.

'It's Berg,' she said simply. 'He was beautiful.'

'Who was Berg?' I said.

'His teacher,' she said. 'No, he wasn't beautiful. But he was always very fastidiously dressed. People dressed up for photographs, of course, but not this one, not in the country or anything.'

There was a pause and I realized she had lost the thread of what she was saying. I asked her who Berg was again.

'Your grandfather's teacher,' she said. 'He was a composer. You knew that. He was a great composer.'

'My grandfather was a great composer?'

'No,' she said, 'Berg was.'

'My grandfather wrote music?'

'Yes,' she said. 'But Mathilde told you that, didn't she?'

I had forgotten what Mathilde had said. It was generally wise.

'Maybe,' I said.

I wasn't a good listener, and I can't remember the rest of what my grandmother said. She told me a bit about Berg, who she was proud to have known. I don't know why she never mentioned it before. It didn't really matter. For a long time she had been claiming that she knew people whom she really didn't know at all. Being in the same city as someone at the same time had long counted as being old friends as far as she was concerned. My grandfather used to keep something of a check on her claims to be intimate with the abdicated King of England or Marilyn Monroe with a terrifyingly vertiginous raise of the eyebrow. Now that he was dead it didn't really surprise me that she was claiming friendship with a long-dead great composer before I had taken my coat off on the strength of a photograph which could have been of anyone. She told me quite a lot about Berg, although nothing really about my grandfather's music. I would have liked to ask, but long experience told me that it was fatal to show any interest in anything my grandmother was saying.

Only one thing really stuck in my mind, and that really more for the way she said it than what she was saying. She said, 'Of course, the worst thing of all is that Helene Berg is still alive and sitting on a great pile of unfinished music of his. She won't release anything. His unfinished works.'

I saw immediately that she was trying to remember or invent some unfinished works and couldn't.

'What are they?' I said. 'Do you know?'

'An opera,' she said. 'Where are you living?'

'In a flat,' I said.

'Alone?' she said. I didn't welcome this curiosity about Vienna, and I let her pour the tea she usually drank, a kind of tea no one else ever had or liked, a tea smelling of perfume and tasting of bark. Mathilde flatly refused to make it.

'No,' I said. 'A man called Archy. He's my teacher.'

'A man called Archy?' she said. I didn't know what to make of this. 'What does he teach you? Singing?'

'Yes,' I said. 'He's my teacher.'

'Oh yes,' she said. 'Your mother said you were living with a girl.'

'So you've seen my mother,' I said.

'Evidently,' she said.

'Yes,' I said. 'I've just moved. I'm just about to move, I mean.'

'What?' she said. 'Which is it to be?'

'I'm just about to move in with my teacher,' I said. I meant that I was moving into my teacher's flat, of course.

'So you're not living with him now?' she said.

'No,' I said. 'I'm moving in later this week.'

'It's as well to be precise, you know,' she said. That seemed to exhaust that for the moment. She took up her cup, drank from it, inspected it for cracks and licked the side, over which tea had spilt. She put it down on the saucer inaccurately, with a crash.

'Who is he, this boy, this man you're living with?' she said.

I regretted saying I was living with him, although I couldn't think of a better preposition. 'He's my singing teacher,' I said.

'Even I have managed to grasp that by now, *du Scheisskerl*,' she said, and the word *Scheisskerl*, which made most people turn away in the street or shield their children's ears as from infection, gave me a familiar warm feeling. 'What is his name and where does he come from?'

'His name is Archy Harcourt and he is English, or perhaps Scottish, I suppose, and his father is an English Lord, I found out,' I said, as if that made it any better, or any sense.

'What is the father's name?' she said.

'Lord of Harcourt, I suppose,' I said.

'Not necessarily,' said my grandmother. 'If his father is a Lord why isn't he a Lord too?'

'I don't know that he isn't,' I said. 'Nor, I suppose, do you.' Perhaps, I thought, he was something else entirely, a Prince or something. I wouldn't have put it past him, though I didn't say so.

'I'm very impressed,' said my grandmother, who clearly was. 'Now you'd better drink your tea and go, if you haven't seen your mother. And thank you for the note.'

I didn't see what she was talking about until I was halfway to the door of the building. 'Goodbye, Mathilde,' I called. There was no reply from the kitchen. Then I saw that she was thanking me for the cheque. Archy used to tell me a story about Chopin. He used to say that Chopin thought of himself as a great gentleman, and when he was forced to take pupils in Paris he hated dealing with money even more than he hated teaching. What he would do was turn to the window at the end of every lesson and talk for twenty seconds about the weather. While he spoke, the pupils were meant to know to put the money on the chimney breast without comment. Archy often talked about the weather, but I don't think he meant me to leave money for him. He first told me this long afterwards, of course. My grandmother was alluding tastefully, if obscurely, to money by using an inaccurate word. I like to think that she felt she ought to say thank you very much indeed, like Frau Egon, but couldn't actually bring herself to use the words.

'Not at all,' I said to the surprised street.

EIGHT

When I saw my mother, I only told her that my grandmother and I were friends again. And that was that. There was no point in saying even that I'd been to the Grünewald to see her. All my mother said was, 'I thought you might be.' She was too busy to concern herself with what people thought of each other, and if she doesn't come up that much in this story, it's only because only the basically idle can afford to spend time thinking about each other and about the dead, plotting revenge and lavishing undeserved love. For most people, who neither teach nor learn nor think about such things, ordinary love and ordinary dislike are all they have time for.

However, it was on the grounds of this that she decided to ask my grandmother round for dinner. When my grandfather was still alive they never went out much to eat. My grandmother had carried on refusing most invitations since, but for some reason she accepted this one. My mother thought she was probably tired of Mathilde's cooking. I was sitting at home and could think of more complicated reasons.

Archy rang me.

'When are you coming back,' he said.

'Tuesday,' I said.

'Not sooner?' he said.

'No, I don't think so,' I said.

'How's the gin?' he said.

'Fine,' I said. 'How are you?'

'Fine,' he said. 'Goodbye.'

'How lovely your home is,' said my grandmother

weirdly. I saw at once that she was determined to be disagreeable. I saw this from her clothes, which were more prinked and infuriated than ever, buttressed with shoulder padding, stiff with hems, shining with buttons in impractical places. It took her four minutes to remove the clothes she wore to intimidate, to repel, and to impress before she reached the alarmingly huge frock she wore whenever she wanted to dominate the conversation.

'How lovely your home is,' said my grandmother again.

'I know,' said my mother shortly. 'Would you like something to drink?'

'I'd like some English gin, please,' said my grandmother with a pointed but not unreasonable glance at Archy's three bottles, sitting untouched on the drinks cupboard.

'There's no gin,' I said. 'Have some beer.'

Three alternatives had presented themselves when I was thinking about the dinner. I could have made something my grandmother didn't like. My grandmother didn't like lots of things, but food wasn't one of them. I quickly saw that a dinner made up of things my grandmother didn't like would not be a dinner worth eating, and would probably rely on the hearts, kidneys and testicles of animals we had never seen, or animals kept about us in our houses. The second alternative was to make something insultingly plain – beans and potatoes, or herrings and bread. This would, of course, have the effect of making my grandmother able to feel sorry for me.

What I did was to cook something so elaborate and layered that it, like my grandmother's dress, would stun and intimidate. I caked long slices of aubergine with salt until the dish they lay in was rippling with the brown Alice-tears of their surrender. I chopped tomatoes and boiled them in oil into viscosity, and then I threw fistfuls of marjoram in, laughing. I fried the aubergine until it was black. I cooked pasta, its steam, like the tomato-steam and the aubergine-steam before it, rising like the aftermath of an haruspication. I cut cheeses. And then, in layers, I assembled the first dish. Secondly there was salmon, fried with sweet red onions and left until only warm in vinegar and gin-scenting juniper. Next I took a stalk of asparagus and wrapped it in a thin slice of raw ham, then wrapped that in a thinner slice of cheese. Around this a long anchovy spiralled, and then a transparently pink tranche of veal, parcelled and infolded. At the end there was a secret pudding, one which when put out looked like a grey cardboard dome. Inside pastry, many hours before, I had put a single lemon and a pound of sugar. Six hours of barely beach-heat made the lemon soft, surrounded its complicated pleasures with an adoring syrup. Cut, it spilled its selfish love yellowly before my speechless grandmother.

'So,' said my grandmother, as I put out the coffee, three glasses, four bottles and piles of six different kinds of almond biscuit.

'So,' I said.

'So, you can cook as well as sing,' said my grandmother. 'Do you still sing?'

'Of course she does,' said my mother.

'Well, they're the things that men notice in women, after all,' said my grandmother.

'What do you mean?' I said.

'Cooking and singing,' my grandmother said.

'It's true,' I said, though I don't know why, since it isn't.

'What do you think about this Lord Archy she's living with as man and wife?' said my grandmother to my mother ungrammatically.

'Nothing, actually,' said my mother.

'I really don't know,' said my grandmother with a sigh practised with Mathilde more than once.

'We're not having sex, you know,' I said.

'I remember how much my father loved music and singing, didn't he?' said my mother. 'He loved to play for Friederike so much. Didn't he?'

'I know,' said my grandmother. 'But all that, all that publicking about. It was nothing to do with it. That wasn't really what music was with him. You never heard him play when he was alone.'

'Yes I did,' I said.

'You never heard him play when he was alone, playing to himself,' said my grandmother. 'That was music. It was *his* music.'

'Why, what did he play?' I said, running through my grandmother's next four or five answers in my mind.

'*His* music, I said. Music that *he* wrote, of course,' my grandmother said.

'I didn't know he wrote music,' my mother said.

'Of course you never knew,' my grandmother said. 'It was his music. It was only for him. Did you know?'

'Yes,' I said, beginning to clear up. 'You told me last week. Is it any good, this music?'

My grandmother looked at me as if I should know the answer.

'A shame no one ever played it in public,' said my mother.

'No,' said my grandmother. 'It's a good thing. It should never be played. And they all begged for it, you know, they all longed to play it.'

'What?' I said. 'Who?'

'Everyone,' she said. 'State opera houses. The Vienna Philharmonic Orchestra. The Berlin Philharmonic Orchestra. The Paris Philharmonic Orchestra.'

My mother and I exchanged looks.

'They begged for it,' she went on, 'and he always refused. And now I've got it all, and it's mine to do with as I choose.'

'How is Frau Egon,' I said.

'She's very well,' said my grandmother. 'The *Scheisskerl*.'

NINE

Once, when I was going through Archy's pockets on an afternoon when I had nothing to do, I found a note in the pocket of a coat he didn't often wear. The note was written on the paper of a hotel in Cairo. It said:

> I know now that I am going to die, and am facing my death with equanimity. Should this be found on my body when the wreckage of the aircraft is sifted, I would say only to my mother that I love her a great deal and am sorry if I have caused her distress by the unpleasant manner of my death. I would only ask her to remember that it was probably worse for me. To my father I have nothing to say, except that I do not forgive him and, in the few moments left to me, I do not expect to.

Archy was very nervous of flying, and had written this in advance, in case the aircraft crashed and he didn't have time to write anything, or had no paper, or his pen failed to work. I didn't understand why he had written it in German, but perhaps he thought German was a more suitable language for thoughts before dying. He often went on about the nobility of the poetry and the language in Wolf or Schumann songs, which made me suspect that he didn't actually pay much attention to what any of them meant. I often thought of introducing the words of one dull Schubert song into another, or singing the lines in reverse order, and see if he noticed.

'My grandmother thinks she was married to a great composer,' I said to Archy when I got back from Berlin.

'What was your grandfather's name?' asked Archy.

'Friedrich Weissmann,' I said.

'Well, he wasn't,' said Archy. 'Did she tell you this?'

'Yes,' I said. 'She said he was a pupil of Alban Berg's.'

'Oh yes?' said Archy. 'Did he really write music?'

'Oh yes,' I said. 'Orchestras from all over the world begged him for his latest symphony or piano concerto, but he just wrote "For my beloved Helga", that's my grandmother's name, on the top and put it into a drawer and forgot all about it. My grandmother's house is full of these manuscripts. That's what she was saying, anyway.'

'Have you ever seen any of these?'

'No,' I said.

'Have you been talking to Charlotte recently?'

'No,' I said. 'Why?'

'No reason,' said Archy. 'Did your grandmother say anything about Berg?'

'A bit,' I said. 'Why?'

'No reason,' said Archy. 'Do you think it's true?'

'It seems a bit unlikely,' I said, 'but only really because it's my grandfather. I dare say all great composers are somebody's grandfather.'

'Not Berg,' said Archy. 'Didn't live long enough.'

'No, I suppose not all great composers. Who is Berg, anyway?' I said.

'Oh, nobody,' said Archy. 'A great composer, that's all. Listen, do you love your grandmother?'

'Not much,' I said.

'Do you love her in the way most people love people they're related to?'

'Oh yes,' I said. 'That's a much easier question.'

'Well, encourage her,' said Archy. 'How did you get on with the gin?'

What made me disposed to believe my grandmother's inherently unlikely story was the detail of all the manuscripts. She kept to the story that her drawers were full of operas and concertos. That stuck in my mind and surprised me, though she didn't often surprise me, because if I was going to claim that my husband was a great composer, I would be very careful to add that he had given up composing, or that the only things he'd written were very short and had, anyway, been destroyed. If you claim that you've got the manuscript of enormous orchestral pieces, sooner or later you're going to have to show them to someone, if you hope to make anyone believe you. I didn't ask to see them, of course.

Anyway, after this conversation with Archy, which we had while eating lunch in the park together, I decided that I had somehow misunderstood, and that she was only exaggerating, as usual. Perhaps my grandfather had long ago written a piece which an orchestra had played, or taken a lesson or two with Alban Berg. A week or two later, though, I had a letter from my mother. She said:

> Yes, you were right. The money does come from your grandfather's family.
>
> Your grandmother still believes that he was a great composer, and even starts to talk about harassing the poor widow of his composition teacher in Vienna. I hope she stops short of this dreadful step. I had a very pleasant visit from Frau Egon yesterday, and I'm afraid we both decided she is completely deranged. I'm sorry to have to say this about her.

I told Archy all this, but he'd lost interest by now, and just went on with my singing lessons. I did whatever he told me. 'Try and sing sitting down,' he said, and I did. 'And lying down,' and I did. And soon I was lying flat on my back, and Archy knelt over me with his hands on my throat, to feel if I was tense or relaxed deep in my neck, and I think now how lacking in understanding I was then. Only once did I wonder about it, and it was when Archy, with his left hand on my stomach, reached up with his right, and lifted the dark hair from my pale face. He wasn't listening to me; he was looking at me; and a twinge of terror was in my stomach, somehow, somewhere.

After I found the letter Archy had written about his impending death, I had to read all his letters. I went through the nine drawers of his desk. Eight were full of papers and forms of no interest and illegible manuscripts in utter chaos. The ninth was full of envelopes sent from England. They were from his father, in Cambridge, and had sloping handwriting. They were all unopened. I opened one of the letters. It was in English, so I couldn't understand it, but this is what it said.

My dear Archy,

You will be pleased to hear that my dealings with the College of Arms are nearly concluded. What I had construed and described as the pettifogging obstructions of a needless bureaucracy proved necessary and proper cautions, and the desired conclusion will be reached before the summer is out.

On another matter altogether, I think you should be made aware, since your behaviour gives no sign that you are likely to come to such an awareness without it, that your failure to answer any letters of mine, and your ceaseless and wilful neglect of such trivial matters as my birthday – behaviour which began with your pointed refusal to write any line of congratulation on my being raised to the peerage two years ago – is beginning to cause a great deal of distress to your mother. I therefore trust that you will make the effort to respond to this letter forthwith.

I hope you are well. I, however, am constantly concerned by my sciatica.

Your loving father,
Harcourt.

I copied this out much later, so I can't say if this was the very one I tried to read in January 1973, but as they were all exactly the same, these letters from Archy's father, it doesn't matter a lot.

The other letters I found by chance on another day. Archy's flat was full of books of the sort my mother used to disapprove of my reading when we weren't on holiday. All of them were five centimetres thick, they all had a title consisting of one word, and their authors generally had a first name, a middle initial and a last name. They all had a picture of a woman wearing gold lurex and shoulder pads on the cover, generally with hands on hips and looking fairly cross. They all made me want to speak English well enough to read them. Inside each of them was, I found, a letter on blue paper, in an upright looped typist's hand. I don't know why Archy kept all these letters, these from his so stupid mother, those from his father which he would never open or look at, but then I don't know why he kept the novels after he'd read them. These letters were also in English, but easier to understand with a dictionary and so on.

> My Darling Boy,
>
> Here is another of those terrible novels you and I love so much, I enjoyed this one terribly. The weather is awful here but I'm sure it's simply wonderful in Vienna. I went to see your father yesterday to sort out the last details. Term started at the university yesterday, all the students look so brown and handsome, I don't know how they can afford to go abroad. I think you ought to write to your father from time to time, it would give him so much pleasure, and he's becoming such a twit about it. Have a lovely time, won't you, I miss you so much.
>
> Your darling
> Mother.

Charlotte paid Archy a visit one day and didn't bother to disguise her disappointment that I was in and he wasn't.

She asked me for money for the electricity bill in a desultory way, and I refused. Then I offered her a drink, and before too long she was running through the familiar old stuff about her and Archy, though not in exactly the same way. This time, for instance, it was *The Marriage of Figaro* Archy had wept with grief at when he couldn't sing the lead role.

'Where was his farewell performance?' I said.

'Covent Garden,' she said.

'And how many curtain calls were there?'

'Eleven,' she said.

'And were you there?'

'I remember very well. I was there, you know.'

I paused. Charlotte looked at me with great hostility.

'How are you getting on, someone like you and someone like Archy?' she said.

'Blissfully well,' I said. 'I like to cook and Archy likes to eat and there are two bathrooms.'

What we both wanted to ask each other was, 'Have you ever or would you ever sleep with Archy?' But we didn't. Instead, Charlotte just remarked that she had forgotten that I was to move in with Archy. This wasn't surprising, since I hadn't told her that I was moving in with Archy, or, for that matter, that I was moving out of her flat. Possibly I did owe her some money for the electricity bill. I couldn't remember using any, however.

'What's Archy's father like?' I said.

'He's a wonderful English gentleman, just like Archy,' Charlotte said. 'They live in a beautiful *house* in the country and another in London. It's their family *house*, of course. Lady Harcourt is very reserved, as you would expect, but Lord Harcourt is a perfect host and quite charming. I spent . . .'

Having gathered only that Charlotte knew the English word for house, and that she clearly had never met either Lord or Lady Harcourt, I said, 'I thought they lived in Cambridge.'

'Cambridge is in the country,' Charlotte said. 'In England.'

'I thought it was quite a big town,' I said. 'And quite industrial. Steelworks and papermills, Archy told me. High unemployment. I don't know whether you know, but it suffers very badly from rioting.'

'Their house is well outside Cambridge, of course,' Charlotte said, leaving.

'Charlotte was here today,' I said.

'Oh, her,' said Archy. 'Your old flatmate.'

'Your old lover,' I said.

'Not really,' said Archy. 'I used to suck up to her, but that's all.'

'You used to suck up to her?' I asked. 'I thought she was supposed to be sucking up to you.'

'She does her best,' said Archy. 'But that's the best way to suck up to anyone. If you get them to suck up to you first it keeps them occupied and they don't notice what you're up to. Sorry, but do you like her much?'

'In a way,' I said, surprising myself. 'She's so predictable.'

'That's true,' said Archy thoughtfully. 'But she's a terrible liar.'

'I think I told you that,' I said. 'I like it, anyway. It's so relaxing not to have to make any effort at all to believe what someone is telling you.'

I put out some meat pie on Archy's plate.

'It's jolly good,' he said after a while.

'The trick is to mash some beans and beer with the meat and put a bit of kidney in five minutes before the end,' I said. I asked myself then, and I still ask myself from time to time now, why I was so ridiculously pleased when Archy enjoyed food I gave him. I never cooked to please anyone but myself before. But in those days, going to buy meat, I found myself wondering what Archy would like to eat, and when I got it right, I felt satiated with my achievement.

'It's jolly good, anyway,' he said. 'Ow ow ow. Sorry.'

'Yes, the potatoes are hot. Why do you say sorry all the time?' I said, curious rather than irritated.

'Why do I say sorry all the time?' he said, yawning with the heat of the potato in his mouth.

'Yes.'

'Shyness, I suppose. Or having a lot to apologize for, you know, would be the sophisticated answer. But I don't really say sorry all the time.'

'Yes you do,' I said. 'But you don't apologize. You only say sorry.'

'I don't understand.'

'You just say the word,' I said, and I said the word, '*Entschuldigung*.'

'Oh,' said Archy. 'I don't quite see the difference. But I like the word. It's such a long word.'

'No it isn't,' I said. 'Not really.'

'I like the effort it takes to say it,' he said. 'I like the way it's so difficult to say sorry in German.'

He looked so pleased to have come up with this that I had to say, 'Not really.'

'All right,' said Archy. 'I just like the noise it makes. I just like its up and down.'

TEN

Every day in Archy's flat I got up and exercised my voice. It was difficult to believe that I wasn't improving daily. I loved so much the noises coming back at me in the quick echo of the drawing room. My voice was like a child I was pregnant with, of huge and already evident health. In some time, I would be able to present the voice for admiration, and for a short time it would be mine, and everyone who saw it would think it was mine. But, too quickly, it would leave me, it would go into the world, it would not be mine, and if I met it or saw it or heard its splendour from far off, it wouldn't be mine and it wouldn't know me. So I was happy to have it within me for now, and I let it shock me sometimes when it leapt to C *in alt*; and not only the walls and the glass, but my ribs echoed and vibrated with the aftershock.

I made these splendid noises to Archy, but although I had never made anything resembling them before, he had often heard them or noises resembling them, and he didn't think much of them. But I liked him not thinking much of me, because it let me take him seriously, which otherwise was hard to do.

He gave me an aria every week. The first week we would sing through it together, inaccurately. The second week I would have learnt it, and we would take it apart, and I would attempt to sing it with Archy prodding my stomach, or with his hands around my throat like a respectable psychopath. The third week we would attempt to perform it, and Archy would give up in disgust. And after that it was my responsibility to take it apart myself and sing it, and beat it into submission and make it mine. Archy never taught me how to sing; but perhaps he taught me how to practise, without knowing that was what he was doing. So each week, at each lesson, there was one new aria, one one-week-old aria, and one two-week-old aria, and the lessons ended always in Archy's rage at my terrible inadequacies, which I enjoyed.

'Oh god,' he said one day.

'It wasn't that bad,' I said.

'It was that bad,' he said.

'You've been listening to it without complaining all week,' I said.

'Surely to god you don't think I listen to you singing if I'm not paid to,' he said.

'Of course,' I said. 'Why were you sucking up to Charlotte?'

'A very good reason,' Archy said.

'You know,' I said, 'it's only good manners to treat your pupils seriously.'

'All right,' he said, looking at me as if no one had ever told him he didn't have good manners. 'She said she knew someone I wanted to meet.'

'Who?' I said.

'You remember the man who's supposed to have taught your grandfather to compose?'

'Yes,' I said, 'but he's dead.'

'Yes, I know,' said Archy. 'But his widow's still alive, and Charlotte said she knew her.'

'And did she?' I said.

'Oh no,' said Archy. 'Of course not.'

I had to admit to Archy that I knew nothing whatever about Alban Berg, which surprised him less than I would have preferred. Archy was not actually a lot of use for finding anything like this out, as he was only interested in music, and not in people in the least. He said that Berg was a great composer, which he had said before, and that he'd begun by being able to write nothing but songs. After a few years of hard work he'd started to write very complicated and, Archy said, beautiful music. I'd heard music Archy described as beautiful before, and his definition was not the same as mine.

Then Archy began to explain about the music, and this I couldn't really understand at all. It seemed that the music was written according to two principles. One was a mathematical principle which everyone understood, which was very clear in Berg's music. I don't know who Archy meant by 'everyone', incidentally. The other was only slowly being understood by anyone at all. Berg was interested in numbers which he worked into pieces which meant particular things. There were also names of people, secret messages, quotations from other pieces of music by other people and from his own music, all the way through his pieces. It seemed that all this actually meant something secret, though it wasn't all understood, and certainly not by me.

'Give me an example,' I said.

'All right,' said Archy. 'There's a string quartet by him called the *Lyric Suite* which everyone knows.'

'Mm-hmm,' I said.

'Charming, delightful, just music,' said Archy. 'When he wrote it, Berg sent a copy of the score to his mistress, a woman called Hanna Fuchs-Robettin.'

'Kind,' I said.

'In the score – in her copy of the score – he'd written out a lot of codes, labelled bits of tune with people's names. About half of it has another part for a soprano singing about their undying love, or something. In other words, the string quartet has a kind of secret shadow. It used to be a secret love-letter in public, but if the soprano sings the words, it's an open love-letter in secrecy.'

'Are you trying to get hold of this?' I said.

'No, no,' said Archy. 'Everyone knows all about it. But the widow's sitting on something much more interesting.'

'The finished opera, you mean, I suppose,' I said.

'The finished *Lulu*,' Archy said. 'You know all this?'

'My grandmother told me,' I said. 'I don't see why you're interested in all this.'

'Because it's interesting,' Archy said. 'Aren't you interested?'

'Up to a point,' I said. 'My singing must be improving.'

'Not in the slightest,' Archy said.

ELEVEN

Two days after this conversation with Archy, which left me completely confused, I had a letter from Frau Egon, the politest woman I ever met. For me, she was just a woman who used to join in with my grandmother when she said I was the new Christa Ludwig, and my grandmother's best friend, and the woman who let on by mistake that my grandmother had deliberately been excluding me from her musical afternoons. I sometimes wondered what my grandmother's musical afternoons became when they stopped having anything to do with music. Perhaps, though the afternoons had continued, they stopped being musical afternoons and started just being a lot of old ladies sitting round for the lack of anything better to do.

But though Frau Egon didn't mean a great deal to me, she seemed to adore me. She wrote that she recalled with great pleasure my beautiful burgeoning voice, and that it was far too long since she had enjoyed its exquisite silvery tones. I could have shown this part to Archy, who had kept his merit as a singing teacher, in my eyes, very largely by maintaining with dogged persistence that I was completely terrible and talentless, and sometimes by refusing to hear me at all, since it depressed him to have to listen to such poverty of ability.

'What are the others like?' I would say.

'Other what?'

'Your other pupils.'

'Oh, far, far worse,' Archy would say.

'There you are then,' I would say.

Frau Egon was coming to Vienna for a few days to

reacquaint herself, she said, with that beautiful city. It would be very pleasant if she could call on me at least once, perhaps even to sample the celebrated excellence of my cooking. It was good to see that, though she gave no sign whatever of enjoying my food, my grandmother had been ashamed of herself enough to praise it to her friends. Rather annoyingly, however, the letter ended, 'Please, do not invite me to stay with you. It would be intruding on you to too great an extent.'

'Frau Egon's invited herself to stay,' I said to Archy.

'Who is she?' he asked. I told him. 'When?'

'Next week,' I said.

'She can't stay,' he said. 'My mother's coming. Do you mind refusing?'

'I do a bit,' I said. 'If it was just my grandmother or someone, but she's really very nice.'

'Well, find somewhere for her to stay,' Archy said.

'Impossible,' I said. 'I haven't the time to go round hotels inspecting bedrooms.'

'Yes, you have,' said Archy. 'Well, ask Charlotte if she'd mind putting her up, then.'

'Charlotte?' I said.

'It's all right,' Archy said. 'I'll ask her.'

And so Charlotte agreed. It struck me that Frau Egon's coming at the same time as Archy's mother was in fact a very good thing, assuming that the four of us could muster some language in common. I had been running through what I could talk to Frau Egon about since I got her letter, and not much had come to mind. All I could remember her saying was that I was the new Christa Ludwig, and praising my grandmother's cakes, which in any case she bought in shops. Nor did I much fancy hanging round the house while Archy and his mother told each other how much they loved each other and indulged in mutual recriminations, the scent of which hung heavy as *Joy* over his mother's letters. If Lady Harcourt and Frau Egon could be enticed into talking to each other about old-womany things like lavender and the cost of living then it might be made more bearable for everyone.

'Does your mother speak German?' I asked.

'No,' said Archy.

Frau Egon seemed delighted to be staying with Charlotte, since she hadn't met her. She told me that Tuesday would suit her very well for dinner, before I had suggested a day at all. As this was the day Lady Harcourt arrived, though, I said that was fine. Frau Egon's politeness made it impossible not to give in to her. After a few perfunctory comments about the excellence of my voice and her happiness at being about to arrive once again in the most beautiful of cities she rang off. I looked hard at Archy's washing machine. Cauliflower soup and liver, I decided.

For the next days, the clouds over Vienna broke and emptied their waters, did their stuff over the steaming streets with a vengeance. Buying food, I scurried from shop to shop, tried on clothes and fingered silks with one eye on the rain. I was looking through a rack of postcards of Vienna when I saw, in the street, Archy. He was walking through the rain with his usual head-down stride, his hands behind his back, quite unlike the damp clumsy coat-gathering scamper with which I followed him. Fifty metres in front of me, he turned into the kind of café no one ever went into except Japanese, with their bright paper shop-bags and their too-big heads, like rich children sitting over cakes on benches, swinging their legs.

When I had got past the flock of dapper waiters half a foot beneath me, fussing tremendously over the puddles, I looked around for Archy. He was nowhere to be seen. I sat down and ordered a coffee and a plum cake, to keep out of the rain for a while. After a moment Archy emerged from the back of the café with a waiter, who led him to a table where an old woman was sitting with her back to me. The waiter gestured approximately and left them. The woman stood up, turning, and I recognized Frau Egon, smiling, delighted, and dry.

They were performing a mantis-like slow dance of recognition and deference, bowing and holding chairs, and did not see me leave the coffee and plum cake and turn and leave, I think. I didn't have the courage to ask Archy about it, as once before I had asked him how he spent his days.

'This and that,' he had said.

'Not at the conservatory, then?' I had said.

'What do you think?' he had said.

So this time I only said that I had seen him on the street, to which he only replied 'Oh yes?' without interest. What would have been the perfect opportunity was something Archy once told me about the English, which is that when they introduce people to each other who don't know each other, they always say, 'Do you know each other?' Archy said that this is because the English think that everyone ought either to know everyone else, or pretend to. In any case, it's rude to assume that they are less likely to know someone than not to know them, which is obviously the case. If, however, you said to two Germans who didn't know each other, 'Do you know each other?' you would be looked at strangely. So when Frau Egon arrived, I just said, 'This is Archy Harcourt, and this is Frau Schmidthofer, and this is Archy's mother, Lady Harcourt,' and left them all pretending not to know each other, which is more or less what I had suspected would happen.

It was more understandable that Archy would treat his mother as if he didn't know her. Lady Harcourt stood in the hallway and looked about her with tight gaze. She was tall, almost as tall as me. Her hair was hard and high, and her shoes clicked as she walked. She was reined-in and lacquered and made-up with powder and paint to look not attractive, not appealing, not even tidy, but impermeable. Her surfaces were like the carapaces of an insect, and if one imagined what she looked like in bed, or before breakfast, one could only think of the soft white vulnerable flesh of an insect torn from its shell. She gazed directly at me as if she did not expect me to look back. She looked at me with distaste, and she looked at the kitchen, littered with choppings and discarded innards with disgust.

As she spoke, her mouth did not open. In conversation she never looked at whoever she was speaking to, but at someone else, or something else. Archy kept surprising me, all through that long week, by saying 'My mother has just asked you . . .' when she had been addressing remarks to him, or to the wall. If she spoke in your direction, she was never speaking to you, and Archy usually answered her. She arrived wearing a hat, and with her belongings in what looked like the hat boxes in movies. When introduced, she offered her hand after yours and turned away from its limp waist-high wave, as if briefly obliged to hold ordure. She shrank from touch, and I could not see how she could ever have been married. I understood, however, that she could easily have been divorced.

Frau Egon, baffled by the handshake, tried walking round Lady Harcourt until they were face to face, all the time saying, 'My dear lady, how pleasant to meet you, what a fine suit you are wearing, what a handsome son you have, did you, I do hope so, have a pleasant journey?' But Lady Harcourt, offended at being spoken to in a language of opulent guttural strangeness, continued to turn away.

The dinner was good, as Frau Egon kept remarking. Lady Harcourt, however, asked for salt and pepper to be fetched. She poured a small pile of salt at the edge of her plate, ground pepper over the whole thing, and then, tasted, left it with a *moue* of distaste. Frau Egon looked hungrily at the food Lady Harcourt was leaving, and then, with a little pity, at her. I just looked at her.

'How do you know Friederike?' said Archy to Frau Egon.

'I am her grandmother's oldest and greatest friend,' she said.

Lady Harcourt said something in English. Archy ignored her.

'Friederike says that she tells lies a great deal,' said Archy with unnecessary and unwelcome boldness. I concentrated on not disturbing the rhythm of my eating.

'She tells lies?' said Frau Egon. 'No, no, not lies. You have misunderstood, I am afraid. That is it, isn't it?'

'Perhaps,' said Archy. 'She says that her grandmother now says to everyone that her husband was a great composer when he was alive. That is a lie, surely? There can't be much doubt about a lie like that?'

'That is true,' said Frau Egon. 'I have heard her say things of that sort. But perhaps she is right in her belief. I know it sounds strange. I do not know whether the Doctor was a composer or not. Perhaps he was. Perhaps he was a great man, as well. How should one know, really?'

'I do not think,' said Archy, 'that Friederike's grandfather was Alban Berg.'

Frau Egon barely paused. 'That is what she says?' she said. 'How funny. She believes herself to be the widow of Alban Berg? That is really splendid, most amusing, you know. She has such a good sense of humour.'

'No she doesn't,' I said. 'Have you heard of Alban Berg, then, Frau Egon?'

'No,' said Archy. 'She doesn't have a sense of humour.'

'Why, how do you know?' I said to Archy. 'You've never met her.'

'I knew it,' said Frau Egon, more or less at random and more or less speaking to nobody in her embarrassment.

I watched Lady Harcourt eat, her sense of style, her sense of how meat was eaten in England and never was in foreign countries, creating a meal of uneatable vileness out of excellence, and watching us watching her, and appreciating all of it.

'No more,' she said to Archy, as I offered the dish of liver to her almost full plate, in English.

TWELVE

For most of the rest of the dinner, Archy sat with the novel he was currently reading next to his plate, while Frau Egon and I talked over my grandmother and Berlin, and Lady Harcourt looked around her with displeasure. Archy's novels were a great source of puzzlement to me; they were all so bad, and he would never enter into a conversation about them where he would either have to defend them or make fun of them. I tried, a few times, to find out why he liked them, but he would never say; and I tried, a few times, to get him to laugh at them, but he never would. The only way to get him to talk about them was to ask him the plots of them. Then he was cosy, and we sat on the sofa and I listened to him talking.

'And then,' he would say, 'she loses all her money because her husband gambles it away in a casino, and the next day he kills himself, and she finds out that he was completely bankrupt. So she sells all her houses to pay off his debts – she doesn't have to, a French count offers to pay them all off if she will marry him, but she won't, and she pays it all off through a sense of honour – and she goes to live in an attic in Paris. And her mother taught her to sew when she was a child, so that's how she earns her living. No one knows that she used to be a rich woman, and she sews dresses even for her old friends, and they don't recognize her. But one day she's waiting for an appointment with an old duchess in the hall of the duchess's town house, and the duchess's son comes through the door, and he stops and looks at her, and although he's never seen her before . . .'

'What's it called?' I said, when he had finished.

'*Precious*,' he said. Or '*Desire*.' Or '*Honesty*.' These simple words, meaning almost nothing in particular. I liked them, and I think Archy did, too.

After dinner Lady Harcourt went to bed, and Frau Egon asked me to sing.

Archy played the piano very badly for 'Deh vieni, non tardar', which is, after all, not difficult. As I sang I watched him, concentrating madly but ineffectually, and Frau Egon, nodding, enjoying it, and I thought how they might never have met before, and never expected to meet again. After that I sang 'Batti, batti, bel Masetto' with a great deal of lubricious eye rolling between Archy and me. It was something I found almost impossible to learn, as the words, asking to be beaten by a phantom and vulgar lover, seemed not just to me but also to Archy, terribly funny and rude. It was only with Archy that I could think of singing these lurid vulgar things, could even think of learning them, since it was always clear that they could mean nothing that wasn't quite harmless, and we shamed ourselves by sniggering together as the aria progressed.

Finally we had a stab at 'Der Erlkönig', which is never sung by women, but, in Archy's opinion, is much more thrilling when it is. Archy had a lot of theories about the insincerity of baritones and tenors in opera, and the sincerity of sopranos.

'The men are all plotting or lying and betraying the women, who are all honest victims or known by everyone to be wicked,' he used to say. 'So no one's going to believe an obvious lot of tripe in a song unless it's sung by a woman.'

'Women can lie as well,' I always used to say.

'Of course they can,' said Archy. 'I know that. But I'm not talking about real life. I'm talking about opera. Which perhaps means that they're better at lying when they do. Because people believe them.'

'Der Erlkönig' came to its very silly end, and Frau Egon applauded violently, bouncing up and down on the sofa, her fat hands making a strange solitary noise in Archy's drawing room.

'You are so much improved, my dear Friederike,' she said, quite out of breath and shining.

'I hope so,' said Archy. 'I really hope so. I would hate to imagine what she would be like if she was any worse than she is now.'

'Oh, this is too bad,' said Frau Egon. 'How can you say such things?'

'Because they're true,' said Archy. As I said, I didn't mind this sort of thing, because I knew that the day Archy started telling me I wasn't too bad, after all, was the day I should have to start to find someone else to teach me singing.

'Please, you are to sing something else, now,' said Frau Egon.

'No, no,' said Archy. 'I'm too tired and she doesn't know any more songs.'

'She knows so many songs,' said Frau Egon, a little outraged. 'At her grandmother's, every week, three new songs, for four and five years. Really very beautiful, even then, you know, but now incomparable.'

'Well, she's probably forgotten them all,' said Archy, but then gave way. I sang the Webern (the second song of three) he made me learn when I first went to him.

'Well, that was very nice,' said Frau Egon. 'But now I have to go. I am sure I do not want to keep Charlotte from her bed, when she is so kindly having me to stay. She may soon be telephoning here and panicking.'

'How are you getting on with Charlotte?' I said.

'Very well,' she said, in a way which rather froze my conspiratorial grin. I wondered what on earth they had been saying to each other to lead Frau Egon to be so abrupt about it. 'Goodbye. It was pleasant to meet you,' she said to Archy. 'Please say goodnight to your poor mother. I hope she, too, had a nice time.'

'Oh, I'm sure she did,' said Archy unconvincingly.

'She looks so much like someone I know,' I said after Frau Egon had gone.

'Who?' said Archy after a moment.

'Frau Egon,' I said.

'Oh yes?' he said.

'I can't think who, though,' I said.

'No?' said Archy, annoyingly.

Every day Lady Harcourt left the flat after breakfast and went shopping. What conversations among her circle of similarly divorced ladies in London she planned to dominate with her tales of Vienna-bought clothes and Vienna-dwelling son I did not care to imagine. She bought clothes in department stores where only Hungarians went. She bought cream-filled chocolates six days before leaving and kept them under her bed. She filed her guarantees of shoes carefully, in case she needed to return them, and every day struggled with availability, hostility, sizes and the German language. Every morning she asked Archy to go with her, and every morning he called her a taxi. Every evening she returned with three plastic bags, the contents of which she decanted into one of the hat boxes.

'What should your mother be called?' I wondered one day.

'You don't have to call her anything,' he said. 'Why do you want to speak to her, anyway?'

'That's not really what I meant,' I said. 'I meant, what is she called now that she's not married to your father?'

'Oh,' said Archy. 'She's still called Lady Harcourt.'

'Why does she keep his name if she doesn't like him enough to keep on being married to him?' I said.

'Useful in shops, I understand,' said Archy.

'Not in Vienna,' I said.

'She doesn't live in Vienna,' Archy said.

'Couldn't she be called Lady Divorced Harcourt or something?' I said.

'Not as useful in shops, I suppose,' said Archy. 'But it's not really fair, I agree. Particularly since she deliberately didn't divorce him until he became Lord Harcourt.'

'I thought he was always Lord Harcourt,' I said.

'No,' said Archy.

'And I thought you were another Lord,' I said. 'Or something smaller.'

'No,' said Archy.

'Frau Egon thinks you're a charming young man,' I said off the top of my head.

'Well, I am,' said Archy. 'Tell her thank you, anyway.'

'I shan't see her again this week, I wouldn't have thought,' I said. 'Particularly not if she's staying with Charlotte. I wonder if that was a good idea.'

'No,' said Archy. 'Now try that again.'

I sang without conviction. I was lying on the floor and Archy had his right foot, without his shoe on, on my stomach and was pushing down gently. We had long ago given up going to the conservatory for my singing lessons, and had cleared a space in the drawing room among all the books and records and hat boxes for me to lie down and Archy to walk on my stomach.

'You should be strong enough for this not to make any difference to your diaphragm,' he said.

I sang, not believing him.

'Why am I doing this anyway?' I said. 'It's bound to make a difference.'

'Oh, you've got to sing lying on your back the whole time in opera,' said Archy. 'All those death-bed scenes. You can't always leap up and sing standing if you're supposed to be practically dead. I think only in Wagner do you get the chance to die standing up. Everyone else I can think of dies flat on their backs. You've got to prepare yourself for every eventuality, anyway, you know.'

'I don't think I want to be an opera singer,' I said. 'I think I want to be a singer in a big pink frock in oratorios.'

'Don't be ridiculous,' said Archy. 'Whoever heard of such a thing? You're going to be an opera singer, because . . .'

And then he left his sentence unfinished. There was a silence in the room, so usually full of noise. We looked at each other long and hard, seeing nothing in each other's eyes. He leant down, and with his long pink English tongue he traced a wet cold line from the joint in my arm, down the inside of my forearm, along the blue veins of my wrist, inside my salty palm to finish on the tip of my third finger. Lying on the hard floor, I stared up at the unfamiliar angle of his features, on which it was hard to find any expression, and felt a tremor of fear and desire and hunger in my stomach. Oh god, I thought. Not again. And I could not see what my thoughts meant by that.

'Because,' Archy said, 'what else is there for you to be?'

I looked at him.

'And now listen.'

And then he told me something I already knew he was going to tell me.

THIRTEEN

'*Lulu.*'

'What?'

'*Lulu.*'

'I don't know what you're talking about.'

'Berg wrote an opera, remember?'

'No.'

'Alban Berg. He wrote one opera which he finished. And then he wrote another which he didn't.'

'And then there was something about his wife.'

'Yes. She's got a third act.'

'A third act?'

'Hang on a second. The third act's finished, but she won't let anyone see it.'

'Like my grandmother. So how does anyone know that it's finished?'

'Because until fifteen years ago she used to let people see it from time to time. That's completely stopped now.'

'And she's got the only copy?'

'No. She's got one copy of it.'

'What?'

'There's another copy.'

'Of the third act?'

'Of the whole thing. Don't tell your grandmother.'

'My grandmother?'

'Yes.'

'Come back to that. Is it finished?'

'Yes. Everything.'

'You said the other one was finished. And if it's finished, why is she hanging on to it?'

'That one's finishable. This is finished, ready for the printer. And no one knows about it.'

'How do you know about it?'

'Never mind. There's one more thing.'

'What?'

'It's completely different.'

'What's different about it?'

'Never mind. It's another *Lulu*, that's all.'

'Where is it?'

'Never mind.'

'Why can't I tell my grandmother?'

'I'll tell you where it is.'

'Where is it?'

'In the piano stool.'

'No.'

'Yes.'

'Can I see it?'

'No.'

'Who did you get it from?'

'I'm not telling you.'

'Turn over. My grandmother.'

'I'm not telling you.'

'I know, you know. You and Frau Egon.'

'Just trust me, just for once.'

'Why? I don't believe it.'

'Well, you won't have to worry about not telling anyone about it, then.'

'Show me.'

'Not yet. Trust me.'

'I don't.'

'Trust me.'

'No.'

'Trust.'

FOURTEEN

I never knew what falling in love was like; never stored up locks of Archy's hair and kept them under my pillow; never, except by chance, acquired photographs of him, and would never have thought of placing them in a locket. The time after my seduction wasn't the blissful incandescent crush girls practised for. Everything was so new I maybe thought it was good. And the time after my seduction was spent not thinking about our time, our life together, not about our happiness, but about our wedding.

We decided to get married so quickly that afterwards we argued about who started the idea. From the beginning, love for us was like a married couple's, a sitcom love of bicker and fondnesses. It seemed like a guarantee of its substance that there was no heat in it. And what we thought about was our wedding. We thought about our wedding too long and too hard, and we never managed to do anything about it. It wasn't really us. It was me, I suppose, who bought the magazines about your perfect wedding, thought about white silk and white flowers and white doves, all carolling a sweet Disney perfection to the skies; and it was me who managed to forget that Archy had a part in it too. But we had to marry soon, although now I can't remember why; and these things can't be had in a hurry. A church couldn't be had. Nor could a state office at the weekend. So we were to marry on a Wednesday morning. I thought for a while about the clothes to wear. I even went shopping for a grand smart dress with Archy. It was unsuccessful, and the dress I eventually bought on my own I had worn half a dozen times by the time we married. And

Archy surprisingly produced a green tweed suit and even had it dry-cleaned, and even arranged for us to go to a smart hotel afterwards for lunch.

We married on a Wednesday morning, with the traffic too evident outside, with nobody there but two pupils of Archy's, who I was supposed to be friends with, but whose names, six months later, I couldn't recall. A bare wedding, and nothing was there except a happiness I can't account for now.

After Archy and I got married, Lady Harcourt wrote me a letter so very abusive that, as they say, for some time all intercourse was at an end. I didn't mind too much. I didn't even mind Archy translating quite a lot of it for my benefit. The phrase 'That enormous woman' kept coming up in it, but I wasn't insulted. I was beyond that. We were to go first to England, to stay with his father in what Charlotte called his *stately home*, and then to Berlin to stay with my mother for a while.

It didn't seem like it, but it was just like a wedding, I think. When my mother found out that we hadn't asked anyone to come, she said that my grandmother was angry. I realized this meant that she was sad about it. Afterwards we went to the hotel, which Archy said he liked, and we ate lunch, salmon and sole and *loup de mer*. Water is the wedding element, and I was happy, and Archy wrote a long letter to place in his pocket in the event of a plane crash. And afterwards we flew to England.

Beneath me were the towering clouds, and below that was Vienna and its jewelled insect-life, and next to me was Archy, who was my husband, who was gripping my hand with nerves, not affection. Everything was too surprising and bright, except the airline food, which we both refused. We drank a bottle of champagne, which we got because Archy flirted with the stewardess before we took off and told her that we had got married in the morning. I could see she didn't believe us, and I suppose it seemed so little true to us that we must have given the air of unsuccessful confidence tricksters. But I suppose she didn't care too much about the airline's champagne, for she gave us a bottle, though we weren't in first class, and it gave the passengers around us a certain cause for grumbling.

In pressurized cabins, in aeroplanes, you have to mentally double the number of drinks you're having, or to put it another way, you have to halve the number of drinks you would normally want. Under pressure you get drunk faster, your body. A glass of champagne has twice the effect of earthbound champagne. A bottle is like two.

For the first days my marriage was like that. Living under pressure, up in the air. Days seemed twice as long, or twice as full, I couldn't decide which. The vegetables seemed greener. England seemed full of delight. It was a pathetic fallacy, I know (one of Archy's favourite jokes), but marriage seemed for a while like a marriage should be, happier, more fulfilling. It should only have seemed more surprising. It was this oxygenated startle with which I felt myself filled and which, I thought, Archy too was filled with, that made me find Archy's father charming.

Lord Harcourt was the head of a part of the university in Cambridge, a college. He was called the Master and lived in what seemed to me great splendour. Rooms high as ballrooms, panelled and footmanned and filled with chain-store furniture. On the walls was a strange collection of paintings. Some were big and abstract and rather worrying, in grey and black and brown on odd-shaped bits of canvas. One looked like mud smeared on glass. When no one but a footman was in the room, I picked at it. It *was* mud on glass. Others were more scary. There was one of a vaguely malformed woman with dangerously pink skin in a bright blue ballgown, under a tree green as neon. It was a painting clearly meant to be hung in the near-dark.

'My mother,' said Archy, necessarily.

Others were of Lord Harcourt, staring thoughtfully into the middle distance behind the painter's left ear, his hand on a bone, or perhaps an apple. The cardboard books behind him, maybe the strange black robes as well, had obviously been filled in by the painter after Lord Harcourt had abandoned his pose and gone. There was a tiresome metal-and-wood sculpture in the middle of the drawing room, which had to be stepped over the whole time. There were a lot of books, but no photographs, of anyone, or anything.

Lord Harcourt was an easy person to talk to, he was so conceited. He showed no interest in anything I or Archy did. All I needed to do to start a conversation was to ask him something, of any idiocy or ignorance. 'What is a Lord?' I would say, or, 'What does linguistics mean?' or, 'Is it easy to get from Cambridge to London?' What he liked best was to talk about his title, which the English government had given him two years before. It seemed that, though he knew nothing about anything except, I suppose, Russian literature, he could go to London and sit in Parliament and make speeches. No one took any notice when he did, of course, so it didn't seem like much to be proud of, but he managed to tell me about it on several occasions.

After I had been out there for a few days, he took me on one side. Archy had gone out for a walk, which is how he spent most of his time in preference to spending it with his father.

'My dear,' he said.

'Dear Lord Harcourt,' I said, making him beam, 'may I ask you a silly question?'

'Of course, of course,' he said.

'How do you get to be a Lord?'

'Well, it is, you appreciate, an honour, a great honour, and I think everyone who receives the honour – I speak of myself – feels themselves unworthy of it. I feel myself unworthy of it,' he said.

'Oh, don't,' I said, though this was the wrong thing to say and he flinched like a horse.

'I regard it,' he went on, 'as not so much a recognition for me as a recognition for this college, for the university and the work I would not have been able to carry out for the last thirty years without the support of my colleagues.'

'Of course,' I said.

'And,' he said, 'a recognition for my family.'

'Of course,' I said, though it didn't seem obvious to me at all. It didn't seem fair, for instance, that the beastly Lady Harcourt should have any recognition whatsoever, let alone that she should hang on to it long after she had left her husband.

'But I cannot say precisely why I was thought deserving of a peerage,' he went on. 'These matters are swathed in mystery. I was delighted, but I could not begin to guess.'

We walked on, and Lord Harcourt continued to talk about himself. I talked to Archy, later, when the footmen were gone and we were left alone with the mud pictures and the neon portraits.

'You have to get on well with the government,' said Archy.

'And that's all?'

'More or less.'

'It must be something more,' I said, for I found it hard to believe that the Queen made people into Lords just for knowing a lot about Russian literature, or just for getting on with the government, and I said so.

'You're right,' said Archy. 'He was the chairman of a committee inquiring into the rights and wrongs of abortion, or premature birth, or antenatal care, or something. They made a lot of recommendations and my father was highly praised in every newspaper and everything they ever did was promptly forgotten about, thank goodness.'

'Does he know anything about it?' I said.

'He does now,' said Archy. 'Don't ask him about it, though.'

Archy spent much of his time in his father's house on the telephone, calling people in Germany. I didn't know what it was all about, however, since all he ever seemed to say was 'Harcourt here' and then 'Yes', 'No' and 'Impossible' repeated for anything between five and twenty-five minutes. At the end he would say something like 'I regard that as an utterly unhelpful suggestion' and put the telephone down. I asked him if he was talking about *Lulu*.

'No, you idiot,' he said. 'You're the only one who knows about it, you know.'

There was no reason to believe him, but I did. I think now that what I liked about the *Lulu* story was that it was something between us, something that for the moment we had for us but, we both knew, would eventually become understood and known by other people, become commonplace, something even we wouldn't talk about, except to say 'Do you remember . . . ?' I liked that. I liked that for the moment it was just for us. I didn't mind that Archy called me an idiot if he wanted to keep it secret. In a way it was instead of love.

'Do you like Betterave?' Lord Harcourt asked me one day, entering quietly while I was picking bits off the mud-and-glass picture in the drawing room. I thought he was asking something culinary or obscene, so I said 'No', to be on the safe side. It didn't, however, matter very much what you said to Lord Harcourt, he always said whatever he had planned to say anyway.

'That's a pity,' he said. 'I'm very fond of it.' He came up to me, and I realized, too late, that he was talking about the mud picture. 'You know,' he went on, 'several years ago now, I went to visit Larissa Lavchenko. The widow of Lavchenko,' he clarified, unhelpfully. 'In the

Soviet Union. She was a most charming lady. I counted myself as one of her best friends until she died. When I went to see her in 1963, it necessitated, I need hardly say, official permission to leave Moscow and travel to her *dacha*. I must add that, as you know quite well, Lavchenko was never in disfavour with the Soviet government, and was, and is, justly treated as a hero of the Soviet state. However. The journey to her home involved a number of train journeys and a long taxi ride. It was on the way back from her home, and I shall not tire you with an unnecessary account of our long conversation, fascinating though it was and might be in another context. It was on the way back that a curious thing happened. I looked beside me at the window. It was caked with mud from the road. And, as I looked at it, it suddenly reminded me very forcibly of my Betterave. And do you know what that reminded me of?'

'Yes,' I said, to vary things.

'It reminded me of my home. It reminded me of England, and Englishness,' he said, sweeping his arm round to include a man employed by the college to dust the Master's furniture, and to include the wood-and-metal sculpture, and Archy, who was sitting on the sculpture and talking on the telephone in German, and the grinning luminescent wife, and the furniture bought from a chain store for a different and a smaller house, and a vase full of chrysanthemums, buoyant as coiffures, which in Germany are funeral flowers.

'And I'm not altogether ashamed to say that, for a moment, in that Soviet taxi, I felt,' said Lord Harcourt, his voice dropping embarrassingly in pitch, 'slightly homesick.'

After that we went to Germany. In my mother's flat, I sat and talked to her about Archy. She was ready to believe anything good I said about him, since on the plane to Germany he had said that he had arranged a job for me.

'I wish you'd told me that you were arranging it,' I said. 'Was that what all those telephone calls were about, then?'

'Some of them,' said Archy.

The job was singing Zerlina in *Don Giovanni* at the State Opera. It sounded very grand. Archy said, however, that it was about the last time that the production could decently be wheeled out, and I shouldn't expect to be singing to anyone except coach parties. Still, in my mother's, and still more, in my grandmother's eyes, after securing this, Archy could do nothing wrong.

'My dear Archy,' said my grandmother, entering. 'My grandson,' she went on, shamingly.

'My dear lady,' said Archy, kissing her hand.

'How clever of you, how splendid an opportunity, how marvellous,' she said. 'I'm sure she doesn't appreciate it, though.'

'Of course I do,' I said.

'I think she does,' said Archy. 'But I don't know whether she'll be good enough for it.'

'Well, you know,' said my grandmother, delighted, 'that had actually occurred to me, as well.'

'What nonsense you both talk,' said my mother, a little cross with my grandmother. But in fact, I was worried about it as well, chiefly, it's true, by the thought of breaking down in giggles as I was asking the Masetto to beat me, but also because I didn't think I could sing it.

'Why didn't you ask me first?' I said to Archy.

'Because you wouldn't have wanted to do it,' he said.

'I don't,' I said.

'There you are then. And now you're pleased that you're going to do it.'

'No, no, not at all,' I said.

'Absurd,' said my grandmother.

'Well, sorry, then,' said Archy.

After that there was no getting rid of my triumphant

grandmother. It wasn't that she was pleased that I had a job. It was just that she was impressed that she had a grandson-in-law who had the ability to produce a job from nowhere, for someone who didn't deserve it. She looked forward, I suppose, to impressing other people. Perhaps she had the hope that he might be able to do something, I don't know what, for her. In any case, she took to arriving unannounced at my mother's flat, to everybody's annoyance except Archy's, early in the morning or late at night, and spending hours chatting with Archy. My mother gave up offering her drinks, or coffee, or breakfast, in the hope that she would be severely but briefly insulted and refuse to come and see us for a week or two. It made no difference, unfortunately. She just wanted Archy.

Once, when we were all there, my mother openly rolling her eyes at me, Archy suddenly said, 'I have heard from Friederike that you remember Alban Berg, the composer.'

'Of course I do,' said my grandmother. 'He was my husband's composition teacher.'

'I am so interested in Berg,' said Archy.

'He was such an interesting and charming man,' said my grandmother. 'Delightful. Amusing, as well, you know, used to tell the wittiest stories about other people. A long time ago, now, of course.'

'Did he talk about music ever?'

'To me, he talked about music,' said my grandmother. 'In private. I learned a lot about his music when he talked about it, you know.'

'In a way,' said Archy, 'I get the impression that not much is known about his music, though it seems strange to say so.'

'You're quite right,' said my grandmother. 'You're absolutely right. And some of the music he wrote is not well known at all.'

'A shame,' said Archy smoothly. 'It should be better known, surely?'

'Possibly,' said my grandmother. 'Although, to those who know it, it gives such considerable pleasure that it would in a way be a shame to share it with those who would not appreciate it a tenth as much.'

'Perhaps,' said Archy. 'Although it would do no harm to share it a little more widely. And those who know it now would still retain their mark on these pieces, wouldn't they? They are pioneers, after all, aren't they, discovering these works, and liking them?'

'Possibly,' said my grandmother, again. 'But what are we talking about? All these things, all these works, they are all published, all performed. They are not kept from the public. If the public does not like them, that is hardly the fault of anyone but the public.'

'You are, as always,' said Archy, 'quite right.'

'You know,' my grandmother said, 'seeing you two together, so much and so evidently in love, reminds me so much of my dear late husband. My dear, did I ever tell you how I came to meet him? He was such a fine young man, and there was no reason why we should ever have met, you know. You see . . .'

Later, much later, I tackled Archy about this conversation, which had given me the uneasy feeling that it had been practised beforehand and then performed for my benefit.

'Oh,' said Archy. 'It was for your benefit, really. I thought it would amuse you.'

'Not much,' I said. 'I didn't understand what was going on.'

'Your grandmother thinks she was married to a great composer. You were quite right. She's been dropping hints all week. She just wants someone to take a bit of an interest and get the stuff performed. I wanted to make her say it all in front of you.'

'Thank you,' I said. 'But you were talking about Berg.'

'In a manner of speaking,' said Archy.

'Have you seen any of the music?'

'No, of course not.'

'Do you think it exists?'

'Well, either your grandmother's under some kind of delusion, or your grandfather was and your grandmother believed him. Or neither of them. Maybe it's all true.'

'Not likely.'

'No, I suppose not.'

'So what about *Lulu*?'

'What about *Lulu*?' Archy said.

'I though you might have mentioned it.'

'No,' said Archy.

'Where did you get it from, anyway?'

'Where I told you.'

'You didn't tell me anything.'

'No?'

'No.'

'Ah well.'

'Where did you get it from?'

'Not telling.'

'Where?'

'Trust me?'

'Not much.'

'Did you like my father?'

'Did you like my grandmother?'

'I liked your mother.'

'I liked your father.'

'Did you like my mother?'

'Not much. Did you like my grandmother?'

'Difficult questions.'

'Who do you love best?'

'Difficult questions.'

FIFTEEN

As Archy said, the production of *Don Giovanni* was on its last tottering legs. It was old enough to attract a few historians of the theatre, who wrote admiring articles about the fraying scenery and the costumes, cracking with any sudden move, in the newspapers. But ancient as it was, it was about a third the age of half the cast. The Don Giovanni was the oldest member of the cast by ten or fifteen years. He quavered and wobbled as alarmingly as the scenery. Every night I watched from the wings as he and the two nasty croaking old women playing Donna Elvira and Donna Anna followed each other round the stage in a slow-motion pursuit. They would come off stage and collapse immediately into armchairs put there for the purpose, which everyone else had to clamber over to make their entrances and no one else was allowed to sit in. When it came to my turn to be seduced, the producer had wisely abandoned the production's original move, in which the Giovanni threw the shrieking Zerlina over his shoulder. Instead, I walked quietly over to him, so as not to startle, and took his hand. When, in return, he placed his arm round my waist, I was supposed to let out a shriek. But, poor old man, he never remembered that I was going to do it, and every night looked so surprised.

The Masetto and a few others treated the event as quite beneath them, but I was quite pleased even to be singing to a lot of Americans in a language none of us spoke. The utter awfulness of the occasion, completed by an orchestra made up of brothers, friends, pupils, lovers and acquaintances of the usual orchestra, meant that I was treated by the critics and audience as if I were the best thing in it. Not that I was any good. I just looked, I suppose, less grotesquely unconvincing. It made me desperately unpopular with the Donna Anna, who thought that the applause was hers by right. On the first night, assuming that the audience was too short-sighted or too foreign to know who they were applauding, she kept returning to the stage and bowing gratefully, until, to the delight not only of the Masetto and me, but also the Giovanni, the gallery lost all patience and greeted her with a resounding and unanimous boo.

Afterwards, I sat on the edge of the stage in my absurd farm-girl fuck-me costume, looking out at the empty auditorium and swinging my legs. Everyone had gone apart from the conductor and me, and he came out into the pit when he heard me. He was a proper conductor who for some reason had been assigned the dreadful *Don Giovanni*. I had the contacts to get into it; perhaps he hadn't the contacts to get out of it. He was the only thing in the orchestra pit which had been recognizable from one rehearsal to the next. Apart from a dog belonging to a deputizing viola player of unusual senility, which seemed to turn up whether his master was there or not. I liked Heinrich because, if he didn't exactly giggle, he certainly twinkled during 'Batti, batti, bel Masetto'.

'Don't do that,' he said as I kicked over an oboist's music stand.

'Sorry,' I said.

'How did you get involved with this?' he said.

'Oh, my husband fixed me up with it,' I said. I didn't see a lot of point in pretending I'd got it through my own merits or hard work.

'Is he your agent?' Heinrich said.

'Not exactly,' I said. 'Why, how did you get involved with it?'

'Ooh, punishment for sins committed in a previous life, I should say,' he said. 'But who's this powerful husband of yours, then?'

'He's called Archy Harcourt,' I said. I kept my own name after I got married.

'What, the Berg man?'

'No, not necessarily. Is he?'

'Teaches at the conservatory?'

'Yes.'

'The Berg man, then.'

It hadn't really occurred to me that Archy had any particular interest in Berg, apart from supposedly having this supposedly very interesting manuscript of *Lulu* and being polite to my grandmother when she wanted to talk about her husband's eminent teacher. I suppose it hadn't occurred to me that Archy was interested in anything very much. Heinrich changed the subject.

'Have you ever sung any modern music?'

'Of course,' I said, thinking of the Webern (the second song of three) which Archy had long ago made me learn.

'Give me your telephone number and we might work something out. Something interesting.'

I went home and told Archy.

'I think I'm going to get another job,' I said.

'What, stacking the shelves at a supermarket?' Archy said. 'Thank god. You were absolutely terrible tonight. I had to leave at the interval.'

'Oh, I know,' I said happily. 'But no, singing. Heinrich asked me if I'd ever sung any modern music.'

'To which you said no, since to my certain knowledge you haven't.'

'To which I said yes, of course,' I said. 'You always say sopranos would be very good at lying, if they ever took to it. And he said he would fix me up with something he said was very important.'

'Meaning a world première in a church in Graz with four relatives of the composer listening to you caterwauling inaccurately, without a shadow of a doubt.'

'Perhaps.'

'There's a letter from my mother for you,' he said.

'Oh yes,' I said. The letters from Lady Harcourt for me had started arriving so regularly that I put them, unopened, with the letters to Archy from his father.

'And one from Frau Egon,' he said. 'A thank-you letter, I suppose.'

'Have you read it?' I said.

'No,' he said. 'Of course not.'

I put the unperfumed, unopened letter from Lady Harcourt with the perfumed, opened letters from her to Archy. Their number was increasing. What the letter from Frau Egon had to say was this:

> Dear Friederike,
>
> What a delight to see you in your new home, and really kind, kinder than I deserve, of you to entertain me to dinner when I was last in Vienna. Your marriage to that nice English boy – what a joy to us all, but to me, too! I have to say, at the risk of embarrassing you, that I certainly *had an idea*!
>
> But however. You recall that you had very kindly arranged for me to stay with your charming friend Charlotte. She is very fond of opera. On several occasions while I was in Vienna she and I would stay up quite late into the night talking over our favourite arias, and I quite missed these conversations on my return to Berlin. The news of your triumph has reached even our secluded life in the green woods of Grünewald. I mean, of course, Zerlina!

'How does she know it was a great triumph,' I said, 'since tonight was the first night?'

'It would have been too late to write,' said Archy, 'if she'd waited for the reviews.'

I promised her, in return for her great kindness, to do her some favour in the near future, and the perfect opportunity now occurs to me. I write to ask, I know, a colossal favour. She, though fond enough of opera to starve herself for a week for a ticket, should not, I feel, have to go to such lengths. To go to the opera in Vienna, to see an old friend of her new friend Frau Egon glory in the beautiful part of Zerlina in that most beautiful of operas, *Don Giovanni*; is that not a pleasure none of us should have to forgo? It is true that she would sacrifice great things for this. Would you, however, make an old lady happy, and her young friend happier still by using your, I know, considerable influence to obtain, however poor, a seat for her for a performance. I know I ask great things. If you were able for however brief a moment to receive her after the performance, I am secure in saying that her happiness would be complete. I am naughty, I know, but if she does come backstage, please do not let her know that it was I who wrote to you with this absurd and excessive request.

'Fuck,' I said. 'Charlotte's put Frau Egon up to writing to me for a free ticket to *Don Giovanni*.'

'She can have mine, and welcome to it,' Archy said.

'I shan't give her one, anyway,' I said. 'She can buy her own.'

Archy wrote a letter for me:

Dear Charlotte,

Friederike's friend Frau Schmidthofer has written to her asking on your behalf about the availability of tickets for *Don Giovanni*. I have asked Friederike, and it seems there are plenty of tickets left for the performance on the 12th. If you go, Friederike would be pleased to see you after the performance, if she has time.

Love,
Archy.

Then I wrote to Frau Egon.

Dear Frau Egon,

It was lovely to hear from you. I got a ticket for Charlotte without any trouble in the front row of the stalls. I hope she enjoys it, and it's a pity you couldn't be there too. If this kind of chance comes up again, promise me you'll try to come.

I meant the last part, actually. Archy didn't believe me. Frau Egon, of course, would subsequently get a letter from Charlotte complaining about my meanness, which she wouldn't believe, since anyone who knew Charlotte in the slightest was aware of what a complete liar she was.

To my surprise, Charlotte actually came to the performance on the twelfth, and actually came to my dressing room afterwards. You couldn't dress in the room; you had to stand outside in your underwear and clamber in and out of the antique dress and the wig in the corridor, trying to see yourself in the mirror, since the room was so small, and used as a storeroom, and the dress I was supposed to wear so big. Watching me try to dress was an endless source of amusement to the various youths who always seem to have something to do backstage at opera houses; the difficulties of dressing made me look, I realized afterwards, an unusually but appropriately rumpled Zerlina.

When I had taken the dress off and gone to perch with a drink on a stall between racks of costumes for other, more favoured operas, there was a timid knock on the door. Charlotte came in and awkwardly tried to kiss me from the other side of a pile of wigs, without a lot of success. Then she sat on the wigs.

'Thank you very much for the ticket,' she said.

'Not at all,' I said. 'Any time.'

'It was so thoughtful of Frau Schmidthofer to write to you,' Charlotte said. 'She's so kind.'

'Yes, I know,' I said. 'You seemed to get on quite well.'

'Oh, very well indeed,' she said. 'She's had such an interesting life.'

'I know,' I said. I was suddenly very tired and really did not want to hear fabrications about the very interesting life of some old lady who, I knew for certain, had spent practically all of it in the Grünewald bickering with my grandmother about which of them looked more like Christa Ludwig.

'And,' said Charlotte, persevering, 'she's so unselfish. Do you know what she's doing now?'

'Yes,' I said.

'She's writing hundreds of letters to conductors and pianists and singers all over the world on behalf of a very old friend of hers.'

'What?' I said.

'This friend, it seems,' said Charlotte, 'was married to a composer who never had anything performed. And he died quite recently with cupboards and cupboards full of the most wonderful music. And Frau Schmidthofer's friend is too shy to do anything herself, so Frau Schmidthofer's writing all these letters. Don't you think that's wonderful, in a way?'

'She hasn't written to me,' I said.

'Perhaps she doesn't think you're famous enough to do anything,' Charlotte said.

'Give her my love,' I said.

I don't know whether I mentioned that Heinrich the conductor was one-legged, but he was. He came in next to ask me to dinner. He had a curious violent swivelling walk which made you wonder where it would end and what he would hit, and from which people turned away as if it were a recent accident. I'm sure he was never asked about it, but he did have an air of wanting to tell you about it. Like Archy, he created expectancy and tension around him, and they should have been friends.

SIXTEEN

'Yes, I know,' said Archy.

I couldn't speak. My mouth was full of food. We were in Heinrich's impeccably uncomfortable flat. Instead of armchairs and squashy sofas, there were two wood and cane chairs, peculiar constructions which let you extend the arms and put your legs on them until you felt about as comfortable as a mother before a gynaecologist. There were two sofas of wood and metal, upright as hedges and hard as stage sofas. The table we sat at was high, and the chairs were low, so like five-year-olds we ate with arms level with our shoulders. Heinrich kept going out to fetch more food, all of which came on plates the size of ashtrays, all of which was middle eastern, none of which was nicer noticeably than any other part. It was during one of Heinrich's absences that I told Archy that Frau Egon was trying to promote my grandfather's music.

'Yes, I know,' he said.

'Watch out for this,' said Heinrich, coming back with a worrying swerve and a grin. He had resisted help. It was squid fried in its ink. 'It turns your turds black, so don't worry, or think you're dying of an internal haemorrhage.'

I had begun to think that Heinrich's promise to get me a job singing modern music would come to nothing. He hadn't mentioned it again, nor had he been more than ordinarily friendly since. He invited us to dinner after the last performance of the terrible *Don Giovanni*, it's true. 'Bring your husband,' he said, casually. I assumed that everyone else in the cast, including the geriatric Giovanni and the applause-hungry Anna, would be there, and so didn't look forward to it much. Surprisingly, we were the only ones invited. Archy was in such a gloom I tried a joke by suggesting that perhaps he was expecting the Commendatore to put in an appearance. It fell a little flat. 'I don't know what you're talking about,' Archy said. 'You do talk a lot of rubbish sometimes.'

First we talked about the *Don Giovanni*, which most people I knew had thought laughably bad. I didn't care, but Heinrich clearly did, so that didn't last. Then the food, which was easy, since there was so much of it, and all so different. Then the middle east, which was hard, since it was so evidently important, and yet none of us knew the faintest thing about it. At one point, Archy said abruptly, 'The key to the whole problem, it seems to me, is Syria,' which was worse than useless. Finally I started asking Heinrich personal questions, which hardly ever fails. All through dinner, as soon as Heinrich disappeared, Archy and I struck up again in furious near-whispers about Frau Egon.

'How do you know?'

'She asked me to help.'

'When?'

'When she came to Vienna.'

'This is a kind of aubergine paste with garlic and coriander.'

'Looks delicious. Do sit down for a second.'

'Just one more moment.'

'And what are you going to do?'

'I'm going to help.'

'You're going to help?'

'Yes.'

'But what can you do?'

'And, finally, I think I *can* sit down for a few moments.'

'Oh good,' said Archy.

Heinrich's attitude to me, which went beyond politeness and well into flirtation, surprisingly enraged Archy.

'No,' he said. 'I don't, to be honest, think that she was the sexiest or most able Zerlina since anyone in particular.'

'But such a conglomeration of talents,' said Heinrich. 'Really, she is such a cook one hesitates to cook for her.'

'She has the reputation of a good cook,' said Archy. 'But then, Germans have low standards.'

Heinrich was prevented by politeness from remarking that he, too, had that reputation, and that nationality.

'In my opinion,' he said, 'people may be divided into two classes. There are people who like food and people who like painting. However many people you know, you hardly ever find anyone who likes both, or who likes neither. It's very curious, don't you think?'

'No,' Archy said. 'It's not curious, because it's obviously not true.'

'My grandmother likes painting,' I said at random, to break into the happy tennis-like to and fro between Archy and Heinrich, and to remind them that I was in the room. 'I used to go with her when I was a child. She only likes some paintings, though. She likes Caspar David Friedrich and she likes Böcklin. It's all very strange. It all looks the same to me. She always used to ask me what I liked, and then she used to tell me what she liked. She used to have a stick which turns into a seat, and she used to sit in front of these paintings she liked, and just sit and say "*Wie schön*" to them, or rather to me. It leaves a mark in the floor, this stick. It's an English thing. It's called a shooting stick.'

'It's called a shoot stick,' said Archy, his eyes closed. 'You've told me that before.'

I looked at him. 'I was just saying what my grandmother used to call it. And I wasn't telling the story for your benefit.'

'Well,' said Archy, 'your grandmother was wrong.'

'And I haven't heard the story,' said Heinrich after a moment. 'Does your grandmother still like painting?'

'Yes,' I said, looking at Archy. I didn't believe him, anyway. It occurred to me that what I had said sounded like the beginning of a funny story. It seemed to me like a story in itself. When I was a girl, I used to like pears which were too hard, snapping off the top with my new hard teeth. No one else ever liked pears as hard as that, apart from me and my grandfather a little. But you couldn't tell people that, they'd expect something more, or something less. In the same way, my grandmother leaving her mark in front of other people's paintings with her shooting stick, or maybe her shoot stick, seemed to me like a story which didn't need anything else much. But Archy and Heinrich were waiting for the surprising rabbit or the wronged husband coming out of a cupboard which would give a few marks in the floor the correct shapeliness of an anecdote.

'Friederike's grandmother,' began Archy, but I could see he didn't really want to talk about her, particularly if he had to talk about her husband.

'Tell me about this modern music,' I said to Heinrich.

'What modern music?' he said.

'Once,' I said, 'you asked me if I ever sang modern music.'

'Yes,' said Heinrich, 'do you?'

'Oh yes,' I said, looking firmly at Archy. 'I thought you had something particular in mind, that was all.'

'Oh no,' said Heinrich, 'not really.'

'Have you ever been married?' I asked him in desperation. But this was a terribly bad idea, since he began to flirt with me. I even welcomed it when Archy began to talk about Berg and the version of the string quartet with a soprano, which Heinrich pretended to be gripped by, and the conversation lasted for the rest of the dinner, which got no noticeably worse.

The next day, however, Heinrich telephoned. He talked to Archy for a while first, and I left the room. I assumed he was calling to elicit thanks for the dinner, and I wished him luck. After a while, Archy called me back to speak to Heinrich.

'I've been talking to Archy,' he said.

'I know,' I said.

'You know what you were saying last night. Modern music.'

'Yes,' I said.

'Has Archy told you about the *Lyric Suite*?'

'No,' I said, wrongly.

'We were talking about it last night, surely,' he said.

'Oh, the string quartet,' I said. 'And the words and the soprano. Yes, I know.'

'All right,' said Heinrich. 'I was thinking about putting it on with the soprano part. It's never been done. Critics from all over the world. Tremendous coup. Fame and fortune. What do you think?'

It seemed like a wonderful idea. I listened to the string quartet, and didn't much like it; but I knew plenty of people did like it. I wasn't ambitious in the slightest, but it seemed like a romantic sort of story, devoting all this time and effort to producing a score which nobody but your mistress would ever see. All week I was very enthusiastic about the idea, though not to the point of actually learning the piece.

Archy didn't think much of Heinrich's plan to perform the *Lyric Suite* with me singing.

'It's a ridiculous idea,' he said. 'It's not meant to be performed. It's a secret piece. It's just for the woman he wrote it for.'

I didn't understand what Archy meant at all, he was so cross with Heinrich.

'Look,' Archy said. 'He wrote it for this woman, and she's had it until now.'

'So what?' I said.

'Take an ordinary boring piece like the ordinary boring *Lyric Suite.*' I must have shown bemusement, because he said 'Or Beethoven's fifth symphony, or the "Blue Danube" waltz. First it's got a composer, who's interesting. Then it's got listeners. How many listeners has Beethoven's fifth symphony had?'

'Lots,' I said, brightly.

'Ten out of ten,' said Archy. 'Are all those listeners interesting?'

'No,' I said.

'You are brilliant today,' said Archy. 'Now look at the *Lyric Suite*. How many listeners?'

'Not so many,' I said.

'That's not the point. There's still lots. Now, not many, or hardly any of these very uninteresting listeners get the chance to be interesting. They just sit there and say at the end, "*Wie schön*" to try and be a tenth as interesting as the very interesting and important composer. They're trying to make a mark on the piece, but not many of them do very well.'

'Mm-hmm,' I said. It was an English noise I had almost mastered and often practised.

'Now how about the *Lyric Suite* which no one knows?' said Archy. 'How many listeners?'

'Lots soon,' I said happily.

'But until now?'

'Oh, none, I suppose.'

'No,' said Archy. 'One. Hanna Fuchs-Robettin hasn't even needed to say "*Wie schön*" about the *Lyric Suite.*'

'Who is she?' I said.

'The woman he wrote it for,' Archy said. 'She's left her mark without even trying. She's the most interesting listener in the world, because she's the only one.'

'Right,' I said brightly. 'Is she still alive?'

'It doesn't matter,' said Archy. 'The point is that until

now the secret *Lyric Suite*'s only had one very important listener, and now it's going to have lots of very unimportant ones.'

'Are you saying that my grandmother ought to give up and put all my grandfather's music back in a drawer?' I said.

Archy looked directly at me, quite startled. 'That's nothing to do with it. That's completely different.'

'Does it matter, anyway, all these unimportant listeners?' I said.

'Maybe not,' said Archy. 'But there's something you ought to see before you start thinking about the *Lyric Suite*.'

'*Lulu*,' I said.

'Got it in one,' he said.

'Which one?' I said.

'Mine,' he said.

'And now maybe it's mine,' I said.

'Maybe it's yours,' he said.

SEVENTEEN

Berg's journal

Step into my life, then, you splendid gentlemen, you dazzling ladies. That *you*, though, must now be changed from a plural to a singular *you*, and, if it were possible, though the limits of German forbid it, from a masculine or a neutral form to a feminine one. Step into my life, then, you. And by *you*, I mean that trembling, tremulous vocative, *Lady*.

For such I know you to be. I, known widely now for my plurality of tastes among women, will reacquire that reputation in the future, in posterity – that *afterness*, that music's echo of preserving Time – in the secret writings and secret signifying numberings of those shadow doubles, the secret scores now lying in the possession of half a dozen women. But those manuscripts, though true to themselves and true to their moment, confess simultaneously a paradoxical mendacity through their concatenation. They contradict. They lie. They are true. But this, the greatest of my secret journals, serves to admit not multiplicity but fidelity. Like the music you see written above these words, it is Protean, changing, drawn from fifty sources, admitting many where one might suffice. Like the music above these words, in truth it is interested in only one thing. Above, you will see that at no moment does Lulu leave the stage, and, if she does, then the characters have naught left to do but chatter nervously about her until she returns. Here, you see that there is one woman, who never leaves my mind's stage, who cannot be named here except by negative. She is not Hanna, she is not Helene, she is not, though parallels extend as tempting as tendrils, Lulu. But let us – let me, rather, for I speak alone and to you alone – let me consider what she is, what you are to be called in these pages, palimpsestically superscribed between those lines of speaking insignificance we call music.

Luise, do you hear me? I speak to you. Do you recall a moment in Vienna? Do you recall the leaves above a café table made translucent and lambent by the spring sun? I sat down where you were already sitting, deep in a book. We spoke. What of, is now vanished. We rose together. We left together.

Was this the first time we met? Was it the last? Memory travels palindromically, from now to then and back again. Call it, then, first the first time, then the last time, and then, finally, as Memory completes its dizzying cortex-ride, the middle-time.

Pink as a sea-shell's inside was the room we were in. You knelt above me, awaiting me. The light, unaccustomed in that room except to the attentions of waiting chambermaids, was it emanating from outside or inside? Was it you or I? Was it your skin or your eyes? I lay supine on that bed while you took a firm pen-like finger and drew my shape in the bed around me, smiling. My body, written in the sheets, I rose up to see; the act of rising destroyed it; I lay back, you wrote it, my body, your tongue pinkly clasped between pinker lips, the delicious fashion, again. I rose to see it, again gone. I, and still more you, are ones whose names are writ in water.

Writ in water, too, this document. What am I doing? What madness, writing all this down on paper, paper which one day will represent the most valuable thing I ever set down. Madness! A letter might not have its own value; a diary entry might be dismissed as a scribble on the margin of my life, marginal to a life itself marginal to the music it produced. But this, this document, how can it be anything but set in stone? Will not the millions wish to read it; will it not ensure your eternity with my opera, my music, my love? Is this, my beloved, what you and I wish for each other? Eternity?

Yes, eternity is before us. But these pages, these enraptured pages are for me alone, and for you alone; and when we are dead; when I am dead, and, afterwards, when you are dead, then perhaps it may be given over to eternity, or destroyed (or both; are they not possibilities which may both come to pass?) and we will not care. So our love is for the moment for us; and one day it will be for him, and for her, and for them, and for everyone who loves music, and water, and air, and perhaps love itself.

How strange we should know each other! Was it a week later? The reckoning of time is apt for the diary-dates of dinners and parties, concerts and committees, though not for love, and never did I enter your name in writing, and only do so now in secret, and in cipher, Luise. A week it was later, you and I faced each other in black and white over red and brown food and thought of how to speak. Another told me of my bad manners in neglecting you. I did not need to neglect, nor to remember you. I recall what I said to you. 'Do you care for music, Frau . . .?' Another's name, I shall not write it here, not yours, not mine, not, unlike Luise, not nobody's. I remember better what you replied. Why should I remember what I said myself, unless it were tied to your reply? How should I forget a single thing you said, if it were granted to me that you said it to me? You said, 'I like music, but I do not understand it well.' Nor I. Why else shore up the ruin of thought, the fragments of harmony with graphs and tables, marking out time, a dyke against the stress and pressure, the ceaseless weary beat of time when my music is there and I am not?

Time passed. I watched that tease, that frump, that other whose name I cannot write, that Herr . . . to your other, you Frau . . ., sitting in black and white over his dinner. I watched him thinking deeply, writing his music. I have taught him everything, and his music plays my music, parodying my music's expression of love for you. He knows it not, but if he did, and if anyone performed his music he would believe himself mocked by receiving financial reward to tell others, secretly albeit, of my love for his wife. He knows it not, and thus it is only I who am cruelly mocked by myself, by my heart's dearest thought given, I knew it as I gave it, to my heart's dearest thought's husband.

It is true. Later I spoke to another of you. He is my dearest friend, but what he said – he is given to taciturnity, communicating but little, and that through music, and that but little – sullied not me, as he intended, nor you, as he may have hoped, but him, and the one he spoke of. He spoke of my wife. It was absurd. I knew not of whom he spoke. You are not my wife, a hateful title belonging only to her who married the man whose only interest in my music is what he can take from it, what he can steal, and you are certainly no longer she, whatever others may think. After a thought, I recalled that he spoke of another, of whom I did not think.

No night had passed since first I met, since first I saw you, when I did not, in my mind, lie with you, whomever I may have lain with in that fiction we term reality. No food had passed my lips without the thought of the food I wanted most to eat, held by your lips, passing into my mind. And yet he spoke of another, with whom he said I lay, and with whom he said I ate bread and drank wine. He was punished for his blasphemy. I shall write a violin concerto about you, which he will unknowingly conduct.

Another, my teacher, the greatest and the worst of us, wrote to me. How appropriate, but I draw no lessons from the fact that one teacher is writing to another of that other's pupil. He knew not of what he wrote. He wrote of my great work. He thanked me for a fragment of my great work, a fragment we do not yet reach though soon we shall, for it is your speech, though I did not know it as I gave it, as it gave itself, to the other pole of my life, my twelve-sided sombre master, selfless centripetal love giving itself to selfish gravitational thought. I did not know who was speaking as I wrote the words below the music. I thought they were Lulu's, or that mad puppet-master's whose words I here finish the work of erasing which long ago I began. But they were yours, Luise. You do not believe me? Believe me.

He is in Spain, that sober master, writing his sober oratorio – he says an opera, but without soprano no opera is staged, and who shall say that a Second Sacrificial Virgin constitutes a soprano? – on the fate of Zion. I think of him, I think of me. In Spain! I could not write. My music would turn to fandango and bolero, to habanera and manzanilla before I had left the train. Here, the very backs of books, grey spines of scores, folded away from me, yet leak into my music. What hope would these frail musics have in cities less unmusical, more contagious than Vienna and Berlin? They would dance mad tarantellas, stung by music not their own. And yet this man, this S. . . (I name no names, if not yours, then *kein anderer auch nicht*) writes his opera where the women crack their castanets before his face and talk above his head, and he produces a counterpoint all his own. Or am I being once more vulgar?

Vulgarian I am, although our dinner companions would not suspect it. S. . . used truly to say it. You said it, more truly, though the context, you recall, refuses repetition. I return to him, to the greatest and nearest of my teachers. I think of his opera. What will it be, this *Moses and Aaron*? All operas called *and* are otherwise lovers, looking for a unity. This is a dialectic. He says it has three acts. I do not believe it. It has two, and he has miscounted. My operas (what could this, this *Lulu* otherwise be called? *Lulu and* . . .!) do not alternate but accumulate around a single central spasm, palindromically circle, ecstatically build and ecstatically trail away. What is our opera called? *Alban and Luise*? Hope is futile, and naming destinies produces ends which laugh in our faces. But hope I do.

Another day. You see above that we have passed Lulu's triumph, dressed *en papillotes* to dance a modish jazz for the Prince and the great Herr Doktor Ludwig Schön. But, erased, do these names signify anything? Does it matter that soon she will speak, that soon her words and yours will coincide, that immediately after she will shoot her Doctor and you – we will not say, not gifted with foresight in either direction, we will not say at just this juncture what you will do. Except that it will be worse than shooting, worse than knives, worse, worse, worse.

Another day, a day for cycling and a day for picnic, unlike Lulu's party for Doctor Schön which (oh, look above, look above) you see has just begun, but curiously suited to its novelettish tone. Happiness seemed tangible, a stuff in the air, solid as eggs. We could have taken it from each other's ears like amateur magicians, we were happy to leave it there. I did not even, though I thought of it, point it out to you. It seemed so easy. You spoke of books, those things I cannot read, just as plays I cannot see, without wishing to erase their stuff, their words, to start again. You said you were happy to leave it there, you were happy that it was there for you to go and quietly look at. I said I wanted to change it, to be there and for others to see that I had been there. For everyone to be there. I listened to what I was saying. I am the least likely of populists. You said that you were happy that you had been there and wished no one to know it. You said that a writer should be secret, that a composer was always secret. And what else is there? You secret reader, you secret listener, did you love something so much that you sacrificed yourself to it? Or was it not that? Did you, perhaps, hate yourself so much that you sacrificed, you were prepared to sacrifice yourself to nothing, to a book, and nothing more?

It was at this juncture that you spoke, and your words were Wedekind's (I no longer care, his name does as well as any other), were mine, were, finally, Lulu's, and were yours, and this is, unerased, without palimpsest, what you said, and I gazed horrified at your transparent unseeing mediation of these words.

Wenn sich die Menschen um meinetwillen umgebracht haben, so setzt das meinen Wert nicht herab. Du hast so gut gewusst, weswegen du mich zur Frau nahmst, wie ich gewusst habe, weswegen ich dich zum Mann nahm. Du hattest deine besten Freunde mit mir betrogen, du konntest nicht gut auch noch dich selber mit mir betrügen. Wenn du mir deinen Lebensabend zum Opfer bringst, so hast du meine ganze Jugend dafür gehabt . . . Ich habe nie in der Welt etwas anderes scheinen wollen, als wofür man mich genommen hat. Und man hat mich nie in der Welt für etwas anderes genommen, als was ich bin.

And that was all. Nothing more. You then were gone, shooting your Doctor Schön (or am I Alwa? or Geschwitz, distanced by possibility and proximated by desire, as in her case by anatomy and, at the moment you see approaching above, by dress?) and not turning back. No jails exist, however, from which you need escape, no Geschwitzes who need contract scarlet fever, take your place. Your cry of *Freiheit* will be an interior one, a necessary avoidance of the melodrama no decent opera can do without.

EIGHTEEN

I put it down and I looked at it.

'Did Berg have any other pupils?' I said. I couldn't look at Archy.

There was a long silence. I looked at the very old and thick sheaf of papers. On the top was a piece of paper with tables of numbers on it. The second sheet was headed by a line of music – twelve notes, without stems, just note-heads. Below, there were more lines of music, all different, all numbered, one to forty-eight. The twenty-third was ringed. The third and the fourth sheet were just the same, with a different line of music at the head. In each case the twenty-third set of notes was ringed. The fifth sheet said, in large, neat, handwriting, of the sort nobody has any more, *Ein Lulu.* And on the sixth sheet the opera began. It was written out in full score, forty-eight lines of music. In the middle of these forty-eight lines, just above where it said *Violin One*, there was a line where it said *Voice.* And it was under here that what I was reading was written. The words began at the beginning and (I turned the great mass of paper to the end) finished at the end. But, in between, there were long stretches where notes continued in the voice part but there were no words. Only here and there could the journal be read.

'Look at the end again,' said Archy.

I looked. There were no gaps in the music. Everything was finished. Everything was perfect. At the very end was written, in huge letters trailing over the violin parts, *mein Engel*, and then nothing.

'Beautiful,' said Archy.

I had to speak to him. I said, 'Archy, where did you get this from? Is it my grandmother's? Did Frau Egon give it to you?' And my leap of thought didn't hit the ground until I had finished speaking. I went on, a little breathlessly. 'I know you met Frau Egon before she came here to dinner. You didn't just talk about my grandfather's music, did you? She gave you this, didn't she? It's my grandmother's, isn't it? It's about my grandmother, isn't it? Why don't you say something for once in your life that I can believe?'

There was a long and a terrible silence. Archy said, 'Why don't you go on reading?'

'No,' I said. 'Answer me.'

'I know you saw me meeting Frau Egon,' said Archy. 'I saw you coming in dripping like an unsuccessful fisherman. I ignored you. I didn't not see you. We talked about your grandfather's music. That's all. That's all.'

'Answer,' I said. 'One thing. Is it hers?'

Archy was silent.

'Whose is it? Where did you get it?'

'I've answered one thing. Other things can wait. Even you can see that.'

In the exact middle of the pile of papers I had left my hand, and to this point I turned, and I continued reading.

NINETEEN

Monoritmica

L. Your name, shorter now, it leaves my mind, your name and its cipher both. Both I invented, both have no existence outside these pages, I hope, I think. You left me. You had no right to leave me, you could not leave me, you creature, you creation, you self-effaced, self-effacing reader (*und jetzt kommt die Hinrichtung*) read by me.

L. Read by me, these marvellous pages, dense with incident, rich in happening, have, I find, a thread, running through the whole, a nocturnal Penelope-work of forgetting, doing its work too well. Begun in haste, in love, continued in misery, written now in rage, it has kept in harmony with the events it talks about. But something lacks.

L. Something lacks, but not in the music. Completion, repletion, ripeness is all in this music. It breathes fulfilment. As I left the satiate rows and graphs I began with, and wrote, with a trembling and an unanxious pen, the upward fanfare of trombones, I knew how true and how finished this work already was. No, not in the music.

L. Not in the music, but in the text. The text you will hear (next year? the year beyond that? and where? Switzerland? England?) is unfinished, omits, leaves spaces and gaps for the memory of the puppet-master. But this text omits still more. It omits the colour of your eyes, the pellucidity of your skin. No writing can encompass it.

L. No writing, only music. But more serious omissions have arisen. What does the reader, what do you (had you forgotten, it was for you, only you?) know of you from these lines? A few externals. Your self-effacement, carried out in reading, you unique and uninserting reader, succeeded too well in life. From my life, as from a text, you vanished.

L. You vanished, and in a manner I have already recounted. Other vanishments follow. My characters (look, look above you – the moan of Schön, the clamour of the Athlete, the gather and relax of the Geschwitz) enter and sing their names. Your motif never ceases, never begins to be sounded. When you read this, you will hear it in the music.

L. But though you will hear it in the music, it is not there, it is not in the echo nor in the presounding hush, it is not in the absences nor in the fullness of music. It is its absence itself you will hear. You enter backwards and leave your name to be not-sung, a silence anyone who knows can hear, which no one will hear who does not.

L. Who does not know will not hear you. But who knows will see you entering, unknown to your belief in self-effacement, with your back to them, not seeing them, not knowing them to be there, not knowing in the fullness of your absorption in this *Lulu* that you may turn and see them there, and though you are absorbed in it, it does not contain you.

L. It does not contain you, but your absence. And if I say *they*, those who, like Moses, see only your back parts, who I mean is *I*. There are only two here, you and I, and you are not your own reader, and I am not a reader at all. *Lulu* absorbs you, and I absorb *Lulu*. And, as I said, perhaps now to myself, *und jetzt kommt die Hinrichtung*.

L. And now comes the remainder of the story. You had wondered how you returned to Vienna, as perhaps you wondered then how you were to return to Vienna. I wondered too, and I looked about me. A pool, a knife. Everything I needed. You know the rest, because you know nothing else now, nothing except the plots of my operas.

L. The plots of my operas perhaps plotted how it

happened, or perhaps the plots of the operas your husband will one day write. I killed you, you see. Or not. You were my creature in life as in these words. How could killing you take more effort than drawing the skull and crossbones Puccini drew, one morning, his tongue childishly out, at the death of Mimi?

L. The death of Mimi was not, of course, much like yours. If I created you, I could have killed you freely and then brought you back to life. Caligari am I not, nor yet Svengali, but the simple pleasure of destruction might have proved irresistible. That might have been it. I cannot say. A possible construction of what happened.

L. But *what happened* is a question for children which is never answered. Perhaps I killed you, having a freedom over you which readily includes and perhaps, since I wanted, like that childish questioner, just to see what could happen next, encourages the inclusion of murder. But then, I have to say, perhaps I did not.

L. Perhaps I did not, or did. A difficult question. If A, and if B, then therefore . . . But there is only A. Insufficient data, S . . . would say. With A we do our best, and you who unlike most readers, when you read, efface yourself, don't include yourself in that marvellous web of sound, of canvas, of prose, you know now the answer.

L. You know now the answer. I do not. A, if you were my creature, and if B, you are no longer alive, then C, I must have killed you. Perhaps. Or A, if you were my creature, and if B, you are no longer alive, then C, I might have been mistaken in A. Perhaps. You see, you may not be dead. You may have left life. My life.

L. My life is now empty of you. Absorbed in you, like you in a novel or opera, when you were removed my life was emptied. Novelettishly, *you were dead to me*. Were you also dead? I do not know. Did I see you again? I do not know. If I had seen you, I would have seen Frau . . ., perhaps on the arm of Herr . . ., child or score in the other hand.

L. On the other hand, perhaps you were dead. Police, newspapers, concerned conversations about the murder of the wife of the amateur gifted composer would have meant nothing to me, and perhaps did mean nothing to me. I do not know. I always believed you, and only you, and now that you are gone from me, so much is certain, whom shall I believe?

L. Shall I believe even what I write? For whom do I write? Do I write for one who believes me, or for myself, whom I do not believe? If you are dead, whom am I writing for? Whom for? For you? The question, once raised, causes me pause, and perhaps more than pause, perhaps causes me halt, in the vertiginous fear of speaking to quite nothing.

L., the only angel, my only memory, L., *mein Engel*.

TWENTY

I turned back to the central pages where my hand, crumpling with numbness, had left a dent. The inscription *Act II, scene ii* had been crossed over once and in its place the word *Monoritmica* had been written. The journal began again after the long and complicated orchestral interlude and continued until the end of the act. Every three pages or so a large letter L was ringed, marking the start of a new paragraph or the end of an old one. I reached the end of the act and turned over. On a new sheet of paper was written *Act III*. On the page following that, something different started. Act three had characters, dialogue, something about shares and a brothel and Lulu. It was the text of the opera. This continued until almost the end. On the very last pages, the vocal line started without words, then was written the words as I have put them down, the last paragraph, and then a few bars of orchestral music. That was all.

'Will you promise me something?' Archy said.

'What?' I said.

'Don't say anything to your grandmother about this.'

'Why?' I said. 'Because it's hers?'

'No,' said Archy.

'On one condition,' I said.

'What?' said Archy.

'That you tell me where you got it from, and whose it is.'

'No,' said Archy. 'I can't tell you.'

I wasn't about to say that in that case I would tell my grandmother, so I said, 'I don't know why, but you don't tell me anything. I hate it. I am your wife, you know.'

I said that as though it made a difference to anything, and Archy looked at me with great surprise, which I suppose I could understand.

Outside, in the course of these days, the weather was disagreeable in many different and expectable ways. Some days it hailed until your hands and face stung and the gutters and runnels were clogged with tiny round presents, the toy golf balls of the air. The air would thicken into rain, or fog, or sleet, or snow, or between states where names gave out. I sat in the window and looked out at the faulty world, framed by the window into the screen of a faulty television, a crippled vision.

I owned one cook book. I never cooked from books, but from thinking about raw food. Recipes in magazines I always read, enjoying their elaborations, their unnecessary garnishes and probable disasters of their instructions. But I never cooked from these recipes. Sometimes I went into book shops and took a cook book and read a few pages in the book. I would then go home, thinking about what I had read, and some time later something I remembered from the book would surface when I was buying food, and I would find myself cooking something which I had read. It was probably nothing like what I had read. So I only had one cook book, which I bought for reasons which had nothing to do with food, and everything to do with virtue.

Every day now I took this cook book which advertised perfect happiness as your prize. If you cooked every dish in this book, your happiness would be complete and your husband would be yours. I smiled at this, getting bliss with your dumplings. But though I might not be a better person, if I cooked a new dish every day I might at least be a better cook. And so each day at noon I took down the book, and opened it at the marker, which was where I had left it the day before. I turned the page to the next page, the next recipe, the next step. And then I wrote down what I needed to buy.

It seemed right to do it this way, to cook one new thing each day, and no more. It seemed right to do it in order, from page one to page three hundred and something, to make sure that it had all been done. Otherwise chaos would slip in. I'd start going back to ones I'd enjoyed, and skipping others I didn't awfully fancy, until some time later there would be some I hadn't made at all, and others I'd cooked four or five times. And then it wouldn't be a cooking course, or a course in the improvement of morals, but a cook book like any other. I wouldn't be better; I'd only know a little more.

What I wanted to do in this saturating way was a continuation of a secret game I played as a child with my grandfather. It was a vocabulary game, but not much like other, usual vocabulary games. We didn't learn a new word every day, or anything like that. If you do that, you start looking for occasions to call people disingenuous, or describe sunlight or conversation as coruscating. Which is no fun. My grandfather's vocabulary game was different. If we were alone in a room, he or I would say a verb, and the other would have to add things to it to change its meaning. If the first player challenged the addition, then the second player had to explain the new meaning. If he or she could, she or he won the point. If she or he couldn't, he or she lost a point. It was easy, and it was secret.

'Go,' my grandfather would say impishly.

'Go without,' I said.

'Go along with,' he said.

'Go through with,' I said.

'Go out with,' he said.

'Go under,' I said.

'Go under?' he said.

'To drown,' I said. 'My point.'

It was surprising that my grandfather liked this game, since he was by nature taciturn, but he always enjoyed its undemanding expandings, and grinned whenever he won a point, or when I won a point. He never said, 'I love you,' and now he never will. He always kept it to himself, but these grins were enough.

'How did you come to marry grandmother?' I said once.

'She made me,' he said once.

So I cooked my way through the winter, subduing vegetables and flesh in orderly and mannerly ways. I had several lives now. I had a Berg life, where everything was uncertain, and a cookery life, where the geometry and clean colours and lines of everything reassured me. And then there was an Archy life, which I tried not to think about.

TWENTY-ONE

Naturally, I couldn't wait to write to my grandmother to tell her about the manuscript. I didn't tell her much about it. I just wanted to see what would happen. My grandmother wrote back saying that it was good of me to remember her interest in my grandfather's old teacher, and her fond memories of Berg, and that it would give her great pleasure to see the manuscript if she were ever in Vienna. Of course, that was all I said. I wanted to see her reaction. If it was hers, it would be familiar. In my letter back, I mentioned that I was soon going to sing in a concert in which the *Lyric Suite* of Berg would be played in a newly discovered version, and it would be nice if she, and perhaps also Frau Egon, came to Vienna to hear it.

Irritatingly, when I showed Archy my grandmother's letter, he remembered immediately that he had told me not to say anything to her. Normally, he could be relied upon not to remember anything he had told me.

'I thought she'd be interested,' I said. 'After all, it's about her.'

'You didn't tell her that?' said Archy.

'No,' I said. 'All right, I just want to know whether she really did have an affair with Berg.'

'I don't think you'll learn anything much from her,' Archy said. 'After all, the journal looks like something he made up to me. Don't you think we'd know if Berg had killed someone?'

'Maybe,' I said. 'But even if they didn't have an affair, I think it must be her that Berg's fantasizing about having an affair with. Mustn't it?'

'Not necessarily,' Archy said.

'Anyway,' I said lamely, 'I thought she'd be interested.'

'That's a very good reason for not telling someone something,' Archy said. 'It's only people who are uninterested in something who can be relied on.'

'In that case, I don't know why you won't tell me what's going on and where you got it from,' I said.

'Because you're obviously more interested than you think you are,' Archy said.

Then he went out, whether to the conservatory or not I didn't know. I thought about who I would trust with the manuscript if I had been Berg. Not my wife. Maybe Luise, assuming that he hadn't really killed her. Not the other musicians who were either in Spain at the time, or very disapproving of the whole thing. Maybe another pupil, or a pupil's wife. Maybe.

I arranged with Heinrich to have some rehearsals with him for the *Lyric Suite* at his house before the full rehearsals began.

'I'm sick of Archy,' I said, sitting in one of the gynaecologist's chairs.

'Oh dear,' said Heinrich, holding a bright drink and leaning forward in concern. I liked Heinrich so much, he was always interested and easy to talk to, when Archy wasn't there. He always gave you a pink or a green or a sunset-orange drink. They weren't often very nice, but they were pleasant to look at. 'Why?'

'Oh, he's misleading me,' I said, realizing too late that the literal truth sounded like a euphemism.

'He's having an affair?' said Heinrich.

'No,' I said. 'What I mean is, he won't tell me the truth about anything.'

'Is he lying to you?' said Heinrich, still not seeing.

'No,' I said. 'He just won't tell me what's going on, or the whole truth about anything. I keep on asking him, and he won't say.'

I began to see, from the way he was holding his head, that Heinrich thought that what I meant was that Archy was in fact having an affair, but that I wouldn't say so.

'I see,' said Heinrich slowly. 'But do you have any idea what the truth might be, if you ever managed to find it out without Archy telling you?'

'Yes, of course,' I said, perhaps a little impatiently. 'I know exactly what the truth of the matter is. I just worry that Archy won't tell me.'

'Poor thing,' said Heinrich, a little too casually.

What I was saying was, in fact, not true at all. It didn't really worry me that Archy wouldn't tell me anything. I just wanted to know what was going on. In the end I decided to let Heinrich go on thinking that Archy was having an affair, just for the moment. The idea was so ridiculous that I couldn't see how Heinrich could believe it for a moment. It made me see that letting people think what they want to think is the easiest and most honourable way of lying, and the most pleasurable. Heinrich believed me because I was letting him think exactly what he wanted to think. It was so easy.

All the same, I knew that one day fairly soon I would have to tell him the truth.

A kind of madness now took hold of me. I wrote a long letter to Lord Harcourt, ostensibly about the beauty of his home and of Cambridge and the extremely pleasant week Archy and I had spent there. Though Archy had never before been very fond of his father, since he and I had married, he had found himself warming towards him, and it would only take a small gesture on his father's part to make their relationship one of pure unalterable love. Faced with his father, I was sure Archy's cynical exterior would immediately crack, and the little boy within him would beg for reconciliation with his father. Naturally, it made no difference to me, but having finished by asking him not to mention my part in this, I went out and posted the letter, laughing.

TWENTY-TWO

What a day the postman had. A letter from my grandmother and a parcel and a letter from Archy's father accepting the invitation to come and stay arrived simultaneously.

'Your father's written to me,' I said to Archy. 'There's a letter in it for you.'

'Put it in the home of lost causes,' said Archy, deep in *Oil*, a five-centimetre-thick volume about the rise of a talented but mysterious purple-eyed painter to become merely the beautiful wife of a Texas baron, before her past rose up and threatened to destroy her.

'He says he looks forward to seeing me on the thirtieth. I think you ought to open it,' I said. The thirtieth was the date I had suggested.

My grandmother said in her letter that she and Frau Egon, whom she described as a *Scheisskerl* only in speech and not in her letters, would come to the concert if I could get them free tickets and they could stay with me. I couldn't immediately think of any objection to this. It was only later that it occurred to me that this meant Charlotte had convinced Frau Egon that her story about my meanness was true. My grandmother said she would arrive with Frau Egon on the thirtieth.

I looked up.

'He thinks I'm going to forgive him,' said Archy. 'He's completely wrong.'

'What do you have to forgive him for?' I said.

'The whole thing,' Archy said, too angry for eloquence. 'Everything.'

Fortunately, it didn't occur to him to ask whether I

knew anything about it. Busy deluding me, I suppose that he didn't think that I could be deluding him.

To my slight surprise, the letter from my grandmother was enclosed in a big package addressed to Archy. I handed it to him.

'What is it?' I said.

'Your grandfather's music,' he said.

'My grandfather's music?' I said.

'I asked your grandmother to send me some of it some time,' Archy said. 'And we might see about getting it performed.'

'Why?' I said.

'It's interesting,' Archy said. 'There aren't so many pupils of Berg that it's worth leaving great piles of music lying around without looking at it.'

'What is it?' I said.

There were no scissors to hand, and Archy began to bite at the string around the package. I passed him a knife. He took it without a word and cut the string. He began taking the brown paper off. When he had finished there was a small nest of paper and string on the floor.

'Why has she wrapped it like that?' I said.

'She thinks it's precious,' he said.

'Is it?' I said.

'It's a violin sonata,' he said.

'What are you going to do with it?' I said.

'Look at it,' he said.

'Will you get it performed?' I said.

'Possibly,' he said.

'Do you know any violinists?' I said.

'A few,' he said.

'Why do you want to do it?'

'Will you shut up for a bit, please?'

He went to the piano with the music. I left the room, shutting the door quietly.

TWENTY-THREE

The secret of sandwiches is this. You have one dry thing and one wet thing. More, and it becomes too complicated. Less, and it becomes one thing between two pieces of bread. Most people disagree with me, and think that a piece of beef between two pieces of good bread is good enough. It is good. It just isn't a sandwich. The wet and dry theory goes, in principle, like this. Soft cheese (dry) and grapes (wet). Tuna (dry) and cucumber (wet). Beef (dry) and peach (wet). It isn't infallible.

I was eating the sandwich I made before leaving Archy to my grandfather's violin sonata outside the Vienna art gallery. I was thinking about the fallibility and fundamental soundness of the theory, which is, in fact, my mother's, when Heinrich appeared, his face lighting up in a small way with pleasure.

'What are you eating?' he said with polite but understandable distaste.

'Ham and banana sandwich,' I said.

'Sounds delicious,' he said. 'Now throw it away and come and have a more suitable lunch with me instead.'

'Are you going to cook?' I said, thinking about the tension of his carrying pots and dishes.

'No,' he said, looking at me with an odd expression. 'I thought we might go to a restaurant, actually.'

I agreed, although in fact I had almost finished my sandwich, and I hadn't planned to eat anything more. Heinrich had endless ideas about the ideal build of singers, which were basically elaborations on the idea that they should be very fat. He was always offering me food. The look in his eye as he put down dishes and passed bowls of bread wasn't hunger, not hunger for food at any rate.

I had been in the art gallery all morning, sick of Berg, of Archy, of the *Lyric Suite* and the padlock which Archy had now put on the piano stool where he kept the manuscript of *Lulu*, in fear of what I don't know, waiting for what I don't know. Rehearsal had now started for the concert. Heinrich had decided to perform it, not with a string quartet but with an orchestra. It was, oddly enough, the first time I had heard any of Berg's music, and I was aware that what I was hearing was not the real thing. Everything was slightly interrupted by Heinrich's good taste, difficult to fault and yet both too brilliant and a little awkward.

I found the whole thing awfully difficult, and had to work the whole time to get it right. The orchestra sighed and muttered like pantomime demons during rehearsals, and even Heinrich was only patient. It was as embarrassing as singing 'Batti, batti, bel Masetto'. I could hardly bear to sing these secret terrible shy words about some woman who might still be alive. If anyone happened to wander into the practice room, I worked hard at avoiding their gaze. Normally I was just thankful at standing with my back to the orchestra.

So when it didn't occur to Archy that I might be interested in my grandfather's violin sonata, I felt I had to get out and do something quite different. And I went to the art gallery. I knew nothing about what I was looking at. The only galleries I had ever been into were those my grandmother took me into. The only names of painters I knew were ones she knew and liked (Böcklin, Friedrich, Gainsborough) and ones whose names get into newspapers (Michelangelo, Aubrey Beardsley). Sometimes, going round the gallery, I saw a picture I thought I recognized from a reproduction, or I saw a name which might have been a name I knew. When I looked closer, however, I was always wrong. It turned out a different name, or it had a 'the younger' attached to it, making me unsure. Or it might have been a different picture altogether, reproduced on the front of a novel I'd been reading.

All the same, I liked going round the gallery, and didn't just look at the pictures with the small crowds round them, some of which I thought I knew, and some of which I knew I didn't. Some rooms I walked through. Some rooms I looked at every painting, some from distances so close I could no longer see the subject of the painting, and the guards told me to move further away, and I thought how serious and how fond of art I must look. In some rooms I saw a painting I thought I knew, or thought I liked, and looked at that for a while. These I think I was actually enjoying, rather than enjoying thinking how much I was enjoying being in the gallery. They're different pleasures, though easy to confuse, and perhaps not worth separating.

Seeing Heinrich gave me pleasure, though having lunch with him was difficult, since I didn't want to eat anything and he obviously felt he had to disguise his hunger. He suggested an Italian restaurant, but in the end we went to a café where I didn't have to eat too much. He had a sausage, and afterwards had another, joking about his unfashionable taste for Teutonic things. I had pickled herrings and potatoes in mayonnaise. This German lunch, taken because, having suggested Italian food, we didn't feel too guilty about eating these childhood things, was pleasant, was (a word of Archy's) pleasurable. 'And what,' said Heinrich, quoting someone, though I didn't ask who, 'is patriotism, but the memory of good things we ate in childhood?' For me, patriotism didn't enter into it, since I wasn't hungry. But it was good to sit and talk about something other than Berg or my grandfather, though now I can't remember what we did talk about. Heinrich paid for lunch. And afterwards we went to bed together.

Of course, it wasn't a success, though not because of the

fascinating mysteries, the new limbs and considered asymmetry of Heinrich's body.

'He deceives you,' said Heinrich. 'Why not deceive him?'

'I just have, haven't I?' I said.

'Not yet,' Heinrich said. 'Be precise. You might just have done something about which you intend to deceive him. But you haven't yet deceived him.'

'Not a distinction worth making,' I said, although I didn't believe myself when I said it. And, in fact, the old-fashioned euphemism 'I deceived my husband with another man' described accurately how I felt, however inaccurately it described my actions.

'Who is your husband?' said Heinrich, just as he had when we first met. 'Your husband or your lover?'

It was a difficult question to answer, and I said, 'Another distinction not worth making.' Heinrich was always making distinctions of this sort. It was part of his cleverness, and also of his stupidity. Was a woman a mistress or a wife? Was a child angelic or demonic? Sometimes they were distinctions worth making. Archy, however, was neither a lover nor a brother. He was a deceiver, in the literal rather than the old-fashioned sense. He was the unbelieved. And if that tells you rather more about me than about him, I can't help that.

Afterwards I took a taxi home, where Archy was still working in bangs and flourishes and cries as if of pain at my grandfather's violin sonata. I didn't disturb him. And two hours later, a telegram arrived. All it said was 'Friederike, *love* Heinrich'. I didn't mind, but I minded that he thought I wouldn't mind. I made something not complicated but slow for dinner, a *ragù* which cooked for half the afternoon and into the evening in milk and tomatoes. I liked to make it with ordinary or even poor quality meat. Scraps of bacon and meat the butcher thought fit to be boiled for dogs went in; out came an unctuous dark stew. The transformation of rubbish was something I relished;

the idea of doing your best with what you have; the idea that lavishness was optional.

Archy wasn't surprised. I often cooked things which needed thought before. But it was quite out of sequence of my solitary journey through the cookery book, and there was something emblematic in its slow simmering wait, like guilt waiting for an occasion.

'How's the violin sonata?' I said to Archy as he came out of the drawing room, wild-eyed and tousled like a composer in a film.

'Too early to say,' said Archy.

'What did you have for lunch?' I said.

'Nothing,' he said. 'I forgot. How was the *Lyric Suite*?'

'Hard,' I said. If he thought I had been to a rehearsal for the *Lyric Suite*, it might prove a useful alibi at some point, though I doubted that Archy would ever become suspicious or jealous. 'Very very hard.'

'Are you enjoying it?' he said.

'Not much,' I said. 'It's so embarrassing to sing. I want it to be in a foreign language that I could be sure no one likely to hear will understand. Korean or Finnish.'

'Oh, why?'

'It's so silly. And you were right,' I said. 'It's not meant for anyone except this woman. His mistress.'

'Maybe,' Archy said. 'But don't you think it's interesting enough to be heard, even if Berg didn't want it to be heard?'

I looked at him. 'That's not what you said at the beginning.'

'No?' he said. 'Maybe not. I ought to get back to the violin sonata. That was delicious.'

As the week went on, my affair with Heinrich, as I dashingly termed it to myself whenever it occurred to me, receded into something I thought about when nothing better came to mind. It began to seem like a strange incident without anticipation, succession or significance. It seemed so historical after a few days that when I went to a real rehearsal for the *Lyric Suite* I hardly thought of Heinrich as in any way different to the Heinrich I had known and periodically thought of before. When he winked at me, I half put it down to Berg's rather saucy words. His grip round my waist when greeting me, I had to remind myself, was not just his helping himself up on to his leg, not just a characteristic piece of thespian or musicianly effusion.

But the thought of the afternoon after the herrings and sausages, when we kept belching into each other's faces, and had to keep rolling off each other, winded with over-eating, was a pleasant one to revive. I often thought about it when I was singing. There was nothing else to think about, my life was so constrained and there was so little in it which might be expected to hold the attention. I was always in need of thoughts which might hold my attention when I sang. Archy believed that when singing, it was counter-productive to think of plums and spaghetti and so on. You had to think about something else, unconnected with singing. I tended usually to think of not thinking about singing, which was probably no good. The thought of Heinrich, on the other hand, seemed to do the trick, and certainly Heinrich himself remarked on how much my grasp of the phrasing, or the tone structure, or whatever, had improved. He said this in a way which was both cautiously polite and managed to suggest that my having had sex with him was the cause. In a way, I suppose, it was, though not in the way he thought.

Archy, of course, failed to notice anything. If he thought my singing had improved, he kept it, wisely, to himself. It wasn't likely that my attitude to Heinrich had changed at all, and he was sensible enough not to stop flirting with me in front of Archy. Archy's father arrived, with too many suitcases and such unimaginably mean presents for both of us that, really, it would have been better not to bother at all. Apart from working silently on my grandfather's violin sonata, Archy promptly set about devising an elaborate programme for getting rid of his father for as much of the time as possible.

The first strategy was a programme of visits and cultural outings for his father which would hopefully get him out of Vienna for at least five days out of seven from dawn to midnight. Munich, Prague, Marienbad, Vierzehnheiligen; no place seemed too improbably distant, too unlikely an exemplar of mid-nineteenth-century industrial architecture, no train line too prone to breakdowns for Archy to organize an outing for his father.

The second strategy for driving him away, or at least cowing him somewhat, was a grand version of what Archy called, singing it with a little tune, *time-to-go-home*, *time-to-go-home*. I rightly interpreted Archy letting me in on the secret of *time-to-go-home* as a major piece of trust. The more people who knew about it, the less effective it would prove against guests who thought it to be amusing. I immediately saw the value of the strategy and never told anyone. For some time I had been wondering why Archy kept records of Herbert von Karajan conducting the themes of Wagner's operas arranged into marches for military bands, or fantasies by Percy Grainger on English folk tunes for three pianos, or the collected recorded works of Zoltán Kodály.

'Do you remember,' Archy said, 'when Frau Egon came to dinner and she wanted you to sing?'

'Yes,' I said. 'I remember singing "Der Erlkönig".'

'Do you remember what else you sang?'

'Mozart. Something modern.'

'Exactly,' said Archy. He went on to explain the theory of *time-to-go-home* which I had unwittingly performed for Frau Egon. The guest who stays after dinner, and shows no sign of leaving, is allowed two records, or two pieces, before the strategy begins in earnest. First, a piece which is a little tiresome in a confined space. 'Der Erlkönig', battering on in its pointless way, was perfect. Next, something modern and rather dry. Webern. Next, a seriously awful piece of music. Of these, Archy had no end. He told me about, and even showed me, a record of a cello concerto by a man called Benjamin Britten which had never taken more than ninety-three seconds to achieve its end. He said he himself had never heard more than that. I was sworn to secrecy.

Archy's father was treated to a grand, three-day-long version of the strategy. The smile was already slightly fixed on his face when my grandmother and Frau Egon arrived.

'My dear ladies,' he said wearily, Mahler mooning on in the background, a little early in the day.

'My lord,' said my grandmother, echoed by Frau Egon, and, practised and awkward as camels, they incredibly curtsied.

'My dear ladies,' said Lord Harcourt, mostly aghast but also a little pleased. I shut the door in Charlotte's face.

'Friederike,' said Frau Egon. 'Charlotte! She is there, with our bags. Enter, enter, my dear!'

'So sorry,' I said, shaking her hand in Lady Harcourt's manner, turning away as I did so. Archy made no attempt to greet anyone or look anything but displeased.

The evening, and the next two days, were made annoying by my grandmother's determination to act at every opportunity as if she were in the presence of an English Lord. Schooled by her, Frau Egon waited standing, stiff as a footman, while he sat down.

'Just stop it, please,' I said to my grandmother as she was trying to help me in the kitchen.

She didn't bother to pretend she didn't know what I was talking about. 'I'm sure he appreciates it. I see your taste in music hasn't improved.'

'Have you seen Archy's manuscript of the Berg *Lulu*?' I said, conversationally.

'No,' she said unenthusiastically. 'I should like to.'

Altogether, I was glad I had the rehearsals for the *Lyric Suite* to go to.

TWENTY-FOUR

I opened the door at the requesting buzz, and there was a big-nosed violinist with his case under his arm. He looked at me expectantly, like a boy impatient for Christmas. It was after lunch.

'Come in,' I said. He followed me into the drawing room, where Archy was sitting at the piano, striking a pose. The violinist nodded at Archy, and began to unpack the complicated fragile machinery of his instrument from its case.

Once Archy had taken up the violin sonata, which he had in rather a big way, the piece had started to belong to him, and not to my grandfather, and not to me. He told me about it. He talked about its structure, and its inventiveness, and the way it used a dissonant chord to begin the paragraphs, to instigate an irresistibly violent motion, and it meant nothing to me. I nodded, and I asked the right questions, which were what Archy had just said, repeated. But I didn't really understand, and I made myself not understand.

'This marvellous bit,' Archy said.

I nodded. The violinist just carried on rubbing a piece of rosin up and down his bow, looked at us. Archy began to play the piano. There was a long slow moan somewhere deep down, and then a thin piping tune somewhere far above it. Deep down, there was a regular ebb and flow; the tune was uncertain, wandering, accelerating and decelerating. Archy stopped.

'Sorry,' he said, and began to play again. 'Then the violin comes in. Something like this,' and he whistled a few notes, rather approximately.

'It's marvellous,' I said.

'Yes,' Archy said. 'Isn't it?'

'Mm,' I said. I knew there was something else to be said, but I didn't know what it might be. What I liked best about the piece, and maybe it wasn't part of the piece, but only a part of the piece for me, was the way the notes were written in my grandfather's handwriting. I recognized it from postcards, fond letters for me, and acerbic notes he left for Mathilde on the kitchen table. And here it was, repeating the words of another voice altogether, a voice his, and only his, a voice no one ever heard maybe.

'Let's go,' said Archy. The violinist nodded, and began to play. The piece began with the violin alone, a long slow vibrating note, full of promise and waiting. And then the line began slowly to move, bringing the piano in uncertainly. The violinist broke off, and Archy played a couple of notes, and then stopped.

'Again,' Archy said. They began to play again. From time to time, the violinist would stop, and play a phrase again, but in a different way. Archy would say, 'No,' or 'Yes,' and then they would carry on. The piece went slowly from unmoving stillness to a kind of clockwork frenzy. But the less it moved, the more motion seemed implied within it, and when the violinist's bow was flailing and Archy's head was bobbing most, it seemed to me that there was no real movement, that the music was putting all its energies into staying exactly where it was.

I listened carefully, but my grandfather wasn't really there any more. Only in the handwriting. I tried to listen, and it slipped away from me, its subtle moves the description of a game I didn't know the rules of.

The violinist stopped, and played the phrase he had just played, and then played it much slower, in quite a different way. He raised his eyebrows in an exaggerated way at Archy.

'Yes,' said Archy. 'Yes, I noticed that.'

'What?' I said.

The violinist looked at me, without contempt or interest.

'Do you think you could go?' Archy said. 'You can hear the piece tonight, when they all get back from Salzburg.'

I went, the violinist's eyes following me to the door.

'What sort of man was my grandfather?' I said to my grandmother that evening, as soon as she was no longer fat and pale and sweating from her angry journey.

'A good man, I suppose,' she said. 'He never talked a lot. I suppose he left that to me.'

'Yes,' I said, 'I suppose he did.'

'A little like Archy, maybe,' she said. 'Cultured, well mannered, polite, always polite.'

'Cultured, well mannered and polite?' I said, disbelievingly.

'Yes,' she said. 'But you were very fond of each other, weren't you? Surely you remember that about him?'

'Yes, I do,' I said. 'Yes, I agree with you. He was, all those things.'

'I thought for a second you were disagreeing with me about my own husband,' my grandmother said. 'When does it all start?'

'Soon,' I said. We were sitting in the drawing room after dinner, waiting for the others to follow Archy and the violinist in. 'At least I hope so. Would you like something more to eat?'

'I'd like some more of that delicious English gin,' she said, dazzling me with her smile, which wasn't meant for me at all. 'Lord Harcourt, please excuse me.'

'No, no,' Lord Harcourt said, coming into the room like an Armada, 'don't get up. I'm delighted to see that you have a taste for such English things. Gin is such a quintessentially English drink, isn't it?'

'Indeed,' said my grandmother. I poured out an extra glass of the English gin for Lord Harcourt and handed it to him.

'No thank you,' he said. 'In England, you know, we don't drink gin after dinner.'

'But,' my grandmother said, 'I am German, so you must excuse me. I have been meaning to tell you that you really do speak the most beautiful German, Lord Harcourt.'

'It's most kind of you to say so,' said Lord Harcourt, giving no sign that he was aware he had insulted my grandmother and, for some reason of her own, been flattered in return. I put the glass of gin on one side, since I certainly didn't drink it. 'How I look forward to hearing your late husband's violin concerto. I'm sure you must miss him a great deal.'

'One misses everyone,' said my grandmother vaguely, not correcting Lord Harcourt.

'I should like enormously to hear about him from you; it would be fascinating to know about a great composer from the person who knew him best in the world,' he said.

My grandmother, a little surprised, smiled. 'My dear,' she said as Frau Egon came in, smiling, and sat down to listen to the conversation. 'But I think he lives on in his music. My husband, you know. When I hear his music, it is as if I am holding a conversation with him, you know.'

'Have you heard this piece before?' I said. 'This sonata?'

'No,' she said briefly. 'My dear young man,' she said to the violinist, coming in with Archy. The violinist nodded, without saying anything.

'Have you heard the piece?' Lord Harcourt said to me, kindly.

'Yes, I have,' I said.

'And what do you think of it?' he said with an air of patience.

'I like it,' I said. 'It's very nice, I think.'

'Nice,' Lord Harcourt said. 'Really.'

'Yes,' I said. 'It's very nice.'

'It's very extreme,' my grandmother said. 'It sounds like my husband, the way it moves and sounds. But all the same, it's very extreme, very intense.'

'Ah,' said Lord Harcourt, who seemed to understand what this meant. 'That I anticipate it, would be an inadequate expression of the, not hopeful, but trustful emotions I feel; that I cannot wait, need not be said; and, in short, if I may express myself in German as I would in English, not translating but rather transliterating, I literally "look forward" to it.'

I was used to Lord Harcourt's showing off in German, and sometimes used to count his subjunctives so as not to have to listen to what he was saying. But my grandmother had never heard him perform before, and nodded approvingly.

'Well, you won't have to wait too long,' said Archy, who never talked to his father in English. 'I think the other extraordinary thing about it is that it's incredibly well written for the violin.'

'Is it?' I said. 'Is it really so well written for the instrument?'

'Yes,' Archy said, but Lord Harcourt looked at me in the way one looks at someone who knows what they are talking about.

I looked out of the window at the quiet sky, heavy with waiting. Outside there was silence; I had the sense that the sun's flushed afterglow at one end of the sky, and the moon just beginning to show in the pale skin of the dusk sky, I had the sense they were presiding over the patient attention of the elements. I looked outside at the evening, and it was waiting for the music; and I didn't see Archy, sitting down at the piano, and adjusting the stool to be a little higher, and then a little lower, and then to be the height it was originally, where he had set it three hours before. Not seeing my grandmother and Frau Egon, raising their faces to the angle at which they listened to music. Lord Harcourt nodding graciously at no one in particular. Archy scratching his head with some violence. And then, the violinist who, until then had been looking at him sceptically, raised the violin to his big-nosed face, and, together, they began to play the marvellous noises.

TWENTY-FIVE

'Do we have to go to Prague for the day?' Lord Harcourt said in an experimentally rebellious sort of way over breakfast two days later. 'It's quite as pleasant to stay in Vienna and even not to go out, you know.'

'It's entirely your responsibility,' Archy said. 'After all, Prague is possibly the most perfect of all capital cities, you know, and if you simply can't raise the necessary interest to see the most beautiful city in Europe, I think we would understand. And, besides, if you set off now you would have quite three hours in Prague, and you'd almost certainly get back before midnight or one.'

'Well, I certainly shan't go,' said Frau Egon very surprisingly. 'I really think I ought to rest today from going to Munich yesterday. It was terribly tiring, you know.'

'And I was going to say that I was never going to go in any case,' my grandmother said. 'So we'll all stay here and perhaps go for a small walk before dinner, to the end of the street and back.'

Archy went out shortly afterwards, with a great deal of putting his gloves on and brushing his overcoat and straightening his hat.

'I think he's annoyed you didn't want to go to Prague,' I said. 'It's one of the cities he's most fond of, you know, and he's the sort of person who always likes to share things he loves with other people.'

'But we're far too old to go three hundred miles every day,' Frau Egon said. 'You have no idea how exhausting that can be. Besides, I don't think Archy can possibly have been there. He seemed to be under the impression Prague was in Hungary.'

So all day long they sat around the flat doing absolutely nothing apart from reminiscing to each other. I practised as much as I decently could, to irritate them into going out, but it didn't have any effect at all. They just raised their voices. I went out for lunch without saying anything, to the nearest café, so that I shouldn't have to cook lunch for them. But when I came back Frau Egon and my grandmother were fussing with egg whites and cream and red peppers and fifteen separate bowls to cook an omelette of unusual silliness for Lord Harcourt. I left them to it, and went to lie down on the sofa.

When I woke up, it must have been two or three hours later. The back of my neck hurt, and my ankles, from sticking out over the end of the sofa. I didn't move, because on the other side of the sofa, Lord Harcourt was talking to my grandmother.

'Many people, I think,' he was saying, 'would have been unable to cope with an experience so distressing and so deeply personal. And, in the end, although I have nothing short of esteem for her, the painfulness of the sequence of events which led up to our separation makes it impossible for me to regard my former wife with anything which surpasses esteem.'

There was a long pause and a sigh. 'How sad,' my grandmother said. 'It is always sad when two people are driven apart by events like that. But, you know, you must not think that your life is at an end. You must think of starting again.'

'Oh,' Lord Harcourt said. 'You are too kind, dear lady. But I do not envisage my life changing now. I lead a public life, and that should be of sufficient fullness to satisfy me.'

'Oh, but surely, you cannot say that your life will never change,' my grandmother said. 'You are still young.'

'How kind of you to say so,' Lord Harcourt said, as if he thought she said it because she meant it, and was not obliged to say it. 'Really kind. Perhaps, given the return of a certain special person, I think my attitude could be more likely to change than now seems probable.'

'You don't think that your wife might want to marry you again?' my grandmother said, alarmed.

'No,' said Lord Harcourt. 'That is a matter beyond conjecture. Although there have been times when I might have wished otherwise, I think I can now say with absolute veracity that the time when she was my wife is a time now entirely and thoroughly behind me, and were the possibility to arise again, I am entirely satisfied that my emotions would be such as would lead me to remove myself from the situation. No, what I intended by saying that a certain special person might return, was in a sense a more abstract suggestion; a suggestion that perhaps a person might come into my life who would bring to it something, not comparable to what my former wife brought to it, but altogether superior. That is always a possibility, and a possible situation to which I cannot be altogether sure how I would respond.'

There was an immense silence. I couldn't see them, but they must have been staring at each other. The randiness was falling from the air, heavy as hail.

'Perhaps,' my grandmother said eventually, and maybe it occurred to her that she could not be sure I was actually asleep, 'perhaps we should go for a walk.'

'Yes, let's,' Lord Harcourt said.

'Did I ever tell you how my husband died?' my grandmother said.

TWENTY-SIX

‘I’m so sick of Archy,’ I said, a week later. ‘Fucking sick.’

Since getting married to Archy I had become a little better at putting a fucking in sentences when the context called for it.

‘So,’ said Heinrich, bright drink in his hand, bowl of pistachios next to his left leg, just where his right knee would be, ‘tell me about it.’

TWENTY-SEVEN

In my empty house, from which Lord Harcourt and my grandmother and Frau Egon had gone to Lenz, and from which Archy had gone, I don't know where, I knelt before Heinrich and told him everything I had promised Archy not to tell anyone.

'My grandfather died a couple of years ago,' I said. 'And it turned out that he'd been a bit of a composer. We – I mean my mother and I – used to think that he never did anything. He had lots of money, and there wasn't any need for him to work, or anything. But after he died the maid told me that he'd been a composer. I asked my grandmother about it, and it turned out that he'd been a pupil of Berg's, and there was a lot of his music lying around in cupboards. He'd never tried to get any of it performed. I don't know why. It's supposed to be quite good. Anyway, my grandmother got this friend of hers, Frau Egon, to go round and write lots of letters to conductors and performers and all sorts of people. And one of the people she went to see was Archy. I think it was partly because I was living with him that she'd heard of him and perhaps she thought he was more important than he is. You know Archy is interested in Berg and knows about him and stuff. Well, he was quite interested in my grandfather's music and ... No, that comes a bit later. After he'd talked to this woman Frau Egon, he suddenly announced to me that he knew about this other manuscript of *Lulu*. You know the Berg opera? You know there's supposed to be some manuscript of the third act in the widow's possession that she won't let out? Well, Archy announced that he'd got hold of another manuscript, of the same third act, but in some ways much better. No, not just of the third act. That's right. The third act's totally complete in this manuscript, but instead of the first two acts, I mean instead of the words in the first two acts, all that's crossed out and instead there's this journal about this mistress of Berg's, who maybe he had an affair with and maybe he murdered even, but probably he didn't, and from what the journal says, it looks to me as if the mistress might well have been my grandmother, if you see what I mean. I mean she might have been the mistress. I know it seems unlikely, but she wasn't always like she is now, I suppose. You know what she's like now. Archy wouldn't tell me where he got the manuscript from, so I thought that, well, it might have been one of the things lying around with all my grandfather's stuff, since it was probably all about her, and even if it wasn't, it was the sort of thing you might give a pupil to look after rather than your wife. I mean Berg might have. So I wrote to my grandmother to tell her about it, just to see what her reaction was. She didn't give much away. In the meantime, Archy got her to send him some of my grandfather's music. A violin sonata. And a couple of days ago he got a violinist to come to the flat and they performed it. Well, it seemed all right to me. Everyone else couldn't stop crying and telling my grandmother that grandfather had been a great man. The poor violinist had to play it twice for us, and a third time the next day for Archy to record it. Do you know him? I can't remember his name, but all that time, I don't think he said anything. It was really a bit extraordinary. But in the meantime Archy's got rid of the *Lulu* manuscript, and he won't show it to my grandmother, and he won't say where he got it from, and every time I raise the subject, or now any subject, he just walks away. It's absolutely awful. I can't stand it any more.'

'No,' said Heinrich.

'Yes,' I said.

There was a very very long silence.

'What's your grandfather's piece like?' he said.

'It's quite like the *Lyric Suite*,' I said. For some reason I didn't want to tell Heinrich what I thought about the piece. It was as if it was a piece of knowledge which he might be able to use against me. 'Well, a bit. I don't know much about music, you know.'

'Yes, I know,' he said.

'You can hear it if you like,' I said. 'We got the violinist to make a tape of it, you know.'

'Yes, you said. Yes, all right,' Heinrich said.

'Do you want to see this manuscript of *Lulu* as well?'

'Yes, all right,' Heinrich said.

'Well,' I said, rewinding the tape, 'you could if I knew where it was.'

'Never mind,' said Heinrich, 'it doesn't really matter.'

'But the impression I get,' I went on, 'is that in the last few days Archy's forgotten all about it, or he's embarrassed about it, or something. He can't keep it quiet for ever, but I think he's doing his best. Here we go.'

The tape began. I handed Heinrich the music, which was on the music stand on the piano. I kept looking at him throughout, but he didn't look at me, or say anything, except once when at the end of the first movement, he said, 'Do you think you could rewind it, and just play the last couple of minutes again?'

'Why?' I said, not knowing what he was thinking.

'Because I like it,' he said.

The tape came to an end. I said,

'Well?'

'Well,' Heinrich said. 'I don't really know what to say. It's not really much like the *Lyric Suite*. When did he write it?'

'When he was studying with Berg, I think,' I said. 'You're not crying, anyway.'

'No,' Heinrich said. 'Is there more?'

'Cupboards full, apparently,' I said. 'Do you think it's good, though?'

'Christ, yes,' Heinrich said. 'Can you get hold of some more of this stuff?'

'Yes,' I said. 'Not now, though.'

'So how do I know it exists?' he said.

'You'll have,' I said, 'to trust me.'

And in the long pause that followed, I realized how much that sounded like Archy. I could have been more helpful. There was something a little eager about his interest in the violin sonata, and something a little unenthusiastic about his response to the *Lulu* manuscript. He didn't seem much interested by that, didn't probe or quicken. It was impossible to put into words, but I knew what I thought of my grandfather's complicated sonata. It didn't move me in the public way it moved everyone around me. When people wept or sat in a kind of trance at the end of the sonata, I disliked it; it got in the way of what I thought about it, whatever that was. Heinrich just sat, jiggling his empty glass, looking at me, withdrawing his trust from me as I had withdrawn my trust from Archy, before he said, 'Okay,' and got up.

When Heinrich had gone I started to think how long it could be before Archy or Lord Harcourt or the others would come back. I wanted something to fill the time, to occupy me. I wanted different and more interesting thoughts, a different mind. But, as when I tried to think differently when singing, the thoughts wouldn't come. Heinrich, so different from everything else, so apart from the other concerns I couldn't get away from, somehow only professionally and drily concerned with Berg, was tainted by my story. Confessing is supposed to make you feel better, supposed to be cathartic. I ran around the house. I did the deep breathing exercises singers do, and pregnant women; I jumped up and down until the telephone rang with the complaints of neighbours. Archy once explained *catharsis* to me, when I was singing *Don Giovanni* and was being cynical about the epilogue. I wondered at the time what had happened to all that purged emotion. Now I knew. The catharsis had happened to the very air around me, now pure of worry and rage and serene with music. Around me, everything was clear, everything of anger and distress and strain deposited in me. Polluted.

I sat and hugged my knees. Archy would find out. Heinrich, who had said I would deceive him, was right. But the deception, the deception was not in the euphemism, nor in what I had thought it would lie in, the claims of purity, the assurances of continued and sole possession. Deception lay in the confessions of truths permitted by the long-ago and half-remembered sexual exchange, then so clean, so bubbled-off from other lives, now so broken-down and stirred-in. I picked up pens, the telephone, put on my overcoat and took it off again, read recipes, and still I came back to hug my knees and groan, heavy with precipitated shame.

There were three days to go until the *Lyric Suite* concert, and when the concert began, those days were thick in my mouth. Every day, they all disappeared, the old to distant and recommended cities, Archy to his usual places, telling me as he left how I could improve my singing, if it wasn't too late. The concert approached. Heinrich telephoned twice, and I pretended that something was wrong with the telephone and I couldn't hear anyone at the other end. I had made myself deaf. I forbade Archy and the others to come to the rehearsal in the afternoon of the concert. I cooked, and I worried normally about forgetting the words, about no one coming, about getting things terribly wrong or breaking down in a fit of laughter. Everything around me was everyday, was uninteresting, was acceptable. In me, thought burned like paper.

And that was how the concert began. I must have dressed, and walked on stage, and acknowledged applause, and waited to sing. But I only remember beginning to sing. I was inured to other shames, and in my single shame produced those swooping notes, those oxygen-starved, privated words with forceful, unsubtle clarity. Berg's widow did not come, and nobody knew whether Berg's mistress had come. But I could see Archy and his father, and Frau Egon and my grandmother, and I looked nowhere else. The orchestra followed me, an unforgettable frenzy never heard before, and Heinrich's poor broken figure flapped at the roar for no reason, and my ribs and teeth and bones ached and trembled with *fortissimo*.

Over. The music hung in the shocked silence like dust. I looked, and saw that I had grasped one hand in the other's fist, raised both to my chin. In the moment which lasts for ever and for no time at all, before the great shout I did not believe, which sounded like a recording of a crowd, I thought for a moment to be a bellow belonging to the anger I left behind me, I saw my grandmother, far away, thirty rows of seats back, raise and point her fat clapping hands at me. Face upwards, beaded with tears and sweat, she looked at me as if I were no longer her granddaughter. She looked at me as if I were a diva, not in gratitude or surprise or pleasure, but just looking.

I glanced at Heinrich for the first time that day. He was looking at me in a single way, and his expression, which was that of, surprisingly, relief, had no power to affect me. He had forgotten to raise his hand to take me and bow together, and I turned away from him, gathered my black skirts around me, and left the stage, to wait for my grandmother and her old woman's fierce embrace, the embrace of a woman who knows she will not have such strength for long.

When I left my dressing room, my hand held hers

tightly, not hers mine, and my face was quite wet with her tears. All the time, she was telling me the old story, the familiar story I'd heard before about how she met my grandfather. It was as if she had to talk, and there was only one story she could tell. I asked her about him in the dressing room, and she was talking through the corridors in the hall, and standing on the pavement while a concierge tried to get a car for us, and failed, and she was still talking all the way home in the taxi. And that was why, when she and I got home, leaving the others to reach home as best they could, we went to the drawing room and, with a stout screwdriver, and in silence, we forced the padlock of the piano stool, and I gave her the manuscript of *Lulu*.

TWENTY-EIGHT

So I asked her how she came to marry my grandfather. The loudspeaker in the dressing room was just beginning with the next piece, the last piece in the programme, and I turned it down before she started.

'Ach,' she said. 'That's a terribly romantic story, you know. But I must have told you before.'

'Well, maybe,' I said. 'But I like the story, so tell me again, unless you don't want to.'

'All right then,' she said. 'I don't mind. Well, his family wasn't the sort of family I would ever have got to know normally. You know they were very rich. Of course you know. And my family weren't at all. They weren't poor, but they weren't anything but ordinary, good people. My father used to be a kind of clerk. I don't know whether that sort of job really exists any more. But he never thought of himself as being remarkable. The strange thing was he was a very proud man. He never let my mother go out to work, though she would probably have liked to.'

'Why?' I said.

'Well, no reason,' she said.

'Shall we go?' I said.

'Don't you want to get changed?' she said. I was still in my heavy black gown. I felt like something which would never survive outside a greenhouse, an over-developed funerary rose.

'No,' I said. 'I just want to go before anyone else gets here.'

The boys got out of our way, and we swept the corridors like duchesses. 'Go on,' I said.

'Well,' she said, on the pavement outside. 'My mother didn't work, and I think she'd have liked to. Just that she got easily bored, I remember, and I suppose that if she had a job she would have had something to do. She never met anyone at home, and she wasn't someone who could sit around all day just finding things to do. She didn't like to cook, or sew, or anything else. So she just waited for my father to come home, and, when he had come home, she just seemed to be waiting for something else to happen. Something interesting always seemed to be about to happen to her, but it never did. Anyway, he was terribly proud, and was always worried that I would make friends with the wrong sort of children, or pick up some kind of horrible working-class accent. So my father worked as a clerk in the bank your grandfather's father owned. And he knew who your grandfather was, though your grandfather didn't know who he was. Thank you, a taxi will do very well.'

'Yes, thank you,' I said, leaving the concierge holding his puzzled umbrella.

'I think,' she said, 'in the end my father had too many plans for me and I couldn't possibly fulfil them all. In a way he was a snob, though in quite a strange way. It was all completely centred on marriages. He hated the thought that I might marry someone poor, poorer than we were. But he also hated the idea that I might meet someone far richer. Never ever was I allowed to be friends with anyone who was really more than a couple of millimetres different from us. All my friends were the daughters of other clerks in other banks, and they all lived in exactly the same part of Berlin. Because different jobs mean different things, and different suburbs mean a different social position.

'So you see it was a little amazing that we met at all, your grandfather and I. I think it was at a concert. We must have both been about eighteen. I can't think now why I was allowed to be on my own, or maybe I wasn't. I can't remember. Anyway, there was some affair with a programme too few, or another man insulting me – that sort of thing was always happening, one grew used to it. Particularly since, I suppose, I was really at the utmost edge of respectability, and was always told that I had to be so so conscious of it the whole time.'

I relaxed into the familiar story, looking at the rain outside, enjoying everything about the taxi ride.

'So your grandfather saved me from whatever it was, and we got into a conversation. I knew his house and a bit about him from my father. He was really quite amazed that I knew anything about him at all, though really it wasn't surprising. I remember him being incredibly apologetic that he hadn't heard of me or knew who I was. You know those kind of things, those social things, they never meant anything to your grandfather; his only principle when he met people was never ever do anything or say anything which might conceivably cause them any pain. It isn't a bad principle at all. And we agreed to go for a walk the next day.

'You have no idea how momentous that kind of thing was. It was virtually agreeing to marry someone, to go for a walk with them. I liked your grandfather for not being shocked when I agreed. Really, I didn't have any choice. I'd had sad experiences with my parents and my friends and with men, and I knew immediately what they would think of him. There was absolutely no chance that they would ever like him or approve of him, or think anything other than shame that I had found a man so much richer than me, which could only bring shame and discontent on the family.

'So I said nothing to them. I just went out. We talked a bit about the concert. You know, he knew so much about music, but he never tried to intimidate you with what he knew, he always came down and talked with you on the level you could talk at. A bit like Berg was, later on. And that was nice. And the next week we went to another concert together – I remember he paid for me, and we sat in good seats – and arranged to go for a walk the next day. And it became a kind of a ritual.

'Of course after this had been going on for six months – just a concert and a walk every week, nothing more, not really going on at all – of course my mother happened to see us walking together in the park. My father wanted to know who I was to be walking in the park with a man he didn't know, or said he didn't know. Which is a terribly bad thing to say to anyone, but particularly to an eighteen-year-old girl stubborn as a pig and in love with a beautiful handsome rich charming twenty-five-year-old man. So I went to the concert as usual, and instead of agreeing to go for a walk the next day, your grandfather and I decided that he would come to our house and ask my father if we could marry.

'I was worried that once he had seen where I lived he wouldn't want to marry me, but he was good as anything. It didn't occur to him that he would be refused, but my father wouldn't hear of it. Your grandfather I don't think had ever been refused anything in his life before, and he didn't know what to do. He always managed to do whatever he wanted to do. So I think he was thinking of giving up. He just didn't know what else to do. If someone poor refuses someone rich for no reason except stupidity or some principle too peculiar to put into words, it's hard to know what you can do about it. In the end I said we could just run away. I was worried about not getting any money from my parents for the wedding, because I knew they'd been saving up for it, but he didn't mind about that, and it wouldn't have been much anyway. I didn't mind, you know, that my parents probably wouldn't speak to me again, for disobeying them. That was a little strange, because we all believed that you should love your parents best of all. But I didn't mind.

'So we ran away, and we got married, and we came back – we didn't run far, just a mile or two, but it was a mile or two that made all the difference – and I never saw or spoke to my parents ever again. He was sadder about it than I was. I didn't think it mattered a bit. Sometimes I wonder what would have happened if I had obeyed my parents and married someone they found for me. But it's the most romantic story, isn't it? Can you believe it, looking at your old grandmother now?'

'Is that enough?' I said.

But I was talking to the taxi driver, who nodded. We got out, and we stood on the wet black pavement. Me in my huge dress, my grandmother with rain in her eyes and tears on her face.

'Is that enough?' she said.

'Not quite,' I said.

'No,' she said. 'Have you got a screwdriver?'

TWENTY-NINE

'Why did you marry my grandmother?' I said to the ghost of my grandfather.

'She made me,' he said, shaking his head, in my head.

I was a little mad, that week, a little the victim of other people. The concert restored me, put not just Heinrich, but Archy and the others somewhat in awe of me. Even Archy's usual scorn went down a bit, and when he looked at me, I could see something quite new in his eyes, a little respect, and a little more fear. They all could see my strength, could see that there was no point in evading me, in contradicting me, in not answering my questions. Not that I needed any answers. I was full and I emptied myself out into the impressed receptacles of my surroundings. Archy would have told me anything in those few days in his terror which my strength had exposed. He could see there was no point in asking me why I had destroyed the piano stool to get at the *Lulu*, and for a few days he played the piano sitting on a chair he had taken from the kitchen, sullen but not complaining.

Heinrich called round and I spoke to him. He said that it was too late to get me a part in the state opera's production of *Lulu* next season, which was what all the newspapers were eagerly suggesting. What would I sing, said Heinrich, in any case? The Gymnasiast? Geschwitz? Impossible. I lowered my head, as I didn't know what he was talking about. But, he said, he understood that I was likely to be asked to understudy the Lulu. He emphasized how taxing it was, how likely it was that the lead would drop out and I would turn out to have at least one performance to sing. I was not surprised, nor did I respond when he tried to flirt and mention my grandfather's music in the same conversation.

Nothing was beyond me, at that time. But perhaps I did not notice what was going on around me. Things were more interesting than I had supposed, were perhaps not less interesting than I was. Lord Harcourt cornered me, in a mood of self-satisfaction unusual even for him, to tell me how pleased he was that I had managed to bring about a reconciliation between him and Archy. I knew nothing about it, and I doubt that Archy did. It was as if Lord Harcourt had convinced himself that something was the case, and no amount of external evidence or rudeness or incivility or *time-to-go-home* could possibly contradict his faith.

'I would like to take Archy out for lunch, and you, of course,' he said. 'And your grandmother. That would be delightful, if you could think of a good restaurant you would like to go to.'

'What about Frau Egon?' I said, rather demonically.

'Yes,' he said with a little distaste. 'But your grandmother must come, and I know, since she is really very shy, that she will need some persuasion. I know I can rely on you, my dear. Shyness is a feeling I can all too well understand, since I myself suffer terribly from it. I know you will find this hard to comprehend, but only two years ago, giving my maiden speech – I think that is the correct expression, is it not – in the House of Lords, I found myself trembling like a leaf. It must be said, must it not, that any person, however confident, would find themselves at the mercy of nerves at such an occasion on which one may truly be said to be addressing not only the nation, in a manner of speaking, but quite literally the future, posterity, and history. But,' he went on, remembering what he was talking about, 'there is no reason for her not to come out for lunch.'

'Frau Egon?' I said.

'No,' he said patiently, 'your grandmother.'

Frau Egon didn't come, and my grandmother wasn't shy. She giggled and stuffed herself and started girlishly commenting on her own drunkenness almost before we had finished the first bottle. The food, which Lord Harcourt ordered on our behalf, was vulgar and not particularly good. Lobster is an overrated fish. It's irritating to watch people struggle with it and have to feign pleasure. I didn't try, since it hadn't been my choice; though, even if I had had the chance to order something, I think, at that lunch in the gilded restaurant with the hushed waiters and the fish tanks, I would have masochistically ordered something I didn't like in any case.

'Have you travelled much in Germany, Lord Harcourt?' my grandmother said, smiling like billy-o.

'I have seen large parts of both halves of the former Germany, my dear lady,' he said. 'There are many parts of Germany which have an unusual beauty to which anyone of exceptionally artistic temperament would be attracted, although attracted is too weak a word for the passion which would seize any such person, in which class of persons I am sure both you and I, without undue modesty, would place ourselves, on first viewing the mountainous vistas of Bavaria, not to speak of the windswept landscapes of the North-Sea-bordering territories, almost lunar in their inhospitable yet romantic appearance; but the proposition that the parts of a country which one loves best are those to which one attaches a fond memory of friendship and from which one takes away a memory of kind friends, waiting eagerly to welcome one back, is a proposition from which I should not too readily withold my assent.'

I couldn't look at my grandmother, who was grinning and grinning and grinning. Archy and I said nothing, picking disconsolately at boiled lobster like schoolchildren taken out for an unwelcome treat. Anyway, it wasn't for our benefit.

When my grandmother went back to Berlin, she took

not only the tape of the violin sonata and the manuscript of *Lulu* with her, but also Lord Harcourt. She asked him not to return immediately to England, but to come and stay with her in Berlin for an unspecified length of time.

'Surely to god you don't like him?' I said.

'Naturally I do,' she said, bridling.

'Why?' I said brutally. It might well, I thought, be my last opportunity. 'He's a pompous bore and his wife didn't like him, even though she's mad, and his son doesn't like him, even though he's mad too, and I don't like him.'

'I do whatever I wish,' she said grandly. 'And I don't see why I should pay attention to the opinions of you, or Archy, or a woman I've never met or am ever likely to meet. In any case, he's the best sort of person. He's always charming and entertaining, he's had the most interesting life, as you would know if you listened instead of yawning and tittering and galumphing around for no reason. And I wonder if you thanked him properly when he asked you if you would like to come too for that very delicious lunch he gave me.'

'I thanked him,' I said, wondering who the lunch had been for.

'Did you thank him properly?' she said.

'Did you?' I said, leaving the room, or, as my grandmother would say, galumphing.

Lord Harcourt accepted my grandmother's invitation. He spent the next day on the telephone trying to change the date of his return flight, and, if possible, to change it to a return flight from Berlin, without, if possible, paying anything more, and, if possible, being refunded by the airline for any inconvenience caused. He failed, to his evident irritation.

They left a day earlier than planned. Frau Egon stayed placidly for another three days, during which Archy tactlessly kept singing *time-to-go-home* until I asked him to stop. He was convinced that he, or Wagner, or, as he said, the appalling noises I was making (I was learning some more

Berg songs at the time before I started on *Lulu*) had driven them away. I was less sure.

And then we were alone. And it was much the same as ever, I think. Apart from this strange new fear of Archy's, this way in which he looked carefully at me before he told me how bad I was at singing. I looked back levelly, and we didn't talk about it. After two weeks or so of steady caterwauling in the cause of Berg, my mother wrote to me.

> Your grandmother, of course, had a very good time, although it would be a mistake to expect her to confess it. Even from her account, let alone what I read in the papers – yes, the Berlin papers! – the concert was a great success. If only I could have been there. But there will be other and even bigger successes, I am sure.

I skipped a bit.

> This lunacy of your grandmother's . . .

I went back a bit.

> Unfortunately, now I have to tell you some really very disturbing news. Your grandmother came home, as you know, though I wish you had warned me, with your father-in-law. She telephoned me very briefly to say that she was back, and that Lord Harcourt was with her. That was all I heard from her for the next week. I was very busy and didn't wonder about it too much, even when I heard that she had left Frau Egon with you in Vienna, which would normally have disturbed me a little. From Frau Egon I heard this. I don't know why, but even when Frau Egon went on to tell me that she had seen them in the park actually holding hands with each other, it didn't worry me so much. I thought it was harmless, I suppose.
>
> Some time later both of them, your grandmother and the Lord, came round without warning. They told me, of all things, that they wanted to get married.
>
> This lunacy of your grandmother's is really too much. I really have nothing against Lord Harcourt, and I know from

what he has told me that you and he are great friends. But really, I cannot see that they even know each other at all well, or that she is making a decision which could be seen by anyone as anything other than hasty. I know they say they are in love. But they are wrong and senile.

The wedding takes place in three months. It will be very quiet, I hope. You will both come back for it? It would be nice if you could stay a little longer than usual. The one bright spot in the whole affair is that Mathilde, who clearly thinks that her days working for your grandmother are numbered, mutters 'Whore' every time she passes her in the flat. Your poor grandfather.

I don't know why I go on like this about this silly matter. There are more important things. I have been listening to the tape of your grandfather's piece. I do not understand music, as you know, and perhaps it is because he was my father, but listening to it, it does seem to me to be a work of the most extraordinary . . .

I put the letter down. Underneath the text of my mother's letter was the subtext of whether marriage with granddaughter's father-in-law could possibly be construed as incest. I called Archy.

'Yes, I thought so,' he said, annoyingly.

'How?' I said, bluntly.

'Well, couldn't you see for yourself?' he said.

Archy in normal circumstances was very slow to see that sort of thing, often expressing frank incredulity at unsurprising news, so I said, 'No. I thought they were going to have sex. It never occurred to me they would go this far, though. How could you know?'

'I suppose you were busy at the time,' he said. 'With Berg. Oh, that was the week you weren't speaking to anyone. You wouldn't have noticed.'

A letter followed from my grandmother, announcing the news and her happiness in stilted terms. I wrote back, in stilted terms.

THIRTY

Charlotte was sitting with me. She had taken to dropping in from time to time, although now she had given up asking me for the money for the electricity bill.

'That was Heinrich,' I said, putting the telephone down.

'Heinrich?' she said.

'The conductor, you know,' I said. 'That concert you came to.'

'Oh yes,' she said. 'The man with. Yes.'

'The man with one leg,' I said.

'How did it happen?' she said.

'Oh,' I said. 'It was rather a tragic accident. He was conducting the *Ring* cycle once, when he was quite young. And he used to carry all the scores around, just so that he could skip from one opera to another in rehearsal. Anyway, he was preparing this *Ring* cycle, which was always said to have been the greatest performance since the war, the greatest performance of anything ever, practically, and after the dress rehearsal, he was walking from the opera house, deep in thought about the Norns in *Götterdämmerung*, and carrying an enormous pile of scores. He walked out into the middle of the road, and when the lorry hooted at him, the scores were so heavy that he just couldn't run. And that's how he lost his leg.'

'Really?' Charlotte said, and rather surprisingly giggled.

'No,' I said, giggling as well. 'I don't know how he lost his leg, I'm afraid. He's going to England to do a concert in a month or two – I was just telling him to go and see my grandmother and Archy's father. Did I tell you they were getting married?'

'No,' Charlotte said. 'Crikey.'

'Exactly,' I said. 'You didn't guess, then?'

'No,' she said. 'Did you?'

'No,' I said. 'Archy claimed not to be surprised at all, but I don't believe him.'

'I suppose,' Charlotte said, 'that she was putting on a bit of a performance for him when they were both here. I thought that was just the way she was.'

'Not really,' I said. 'She's usually rude to everybody.'

'Does he play the piano for you?' she said.

'Who?' I said.

'Heinrich,' she said. 'Sorry, I was still thinking about him and his leg.'

'Sometimes he does,' I said.

'Is it hard for him, playing the piano?'

'No,' I said. 'I don't think so. Not that he's particularly good.'

'You know,' Charlotte said, 'I used to play the piano.'

'Were you a professional?' I said, meanly.

'Well, yes I was,' she said.

'Why did you give up?' I said.

'Because I wasn't good enough,' she said. This had an unusual ring of truth.

'Would you play the piano for me?' I said.

'Now?'

'Yes,' I said. 'How about this?' And I gave her a bit of *Lulu*, the bit where Lulu sings a proper aria to her husband. Charlotte looked at it for a moment, then nodded and went to the piano with it. She began to play.

'If for my sake,' I began to sing. Charlotte really wasn't too bad, certainly much better than Heinrich.

'You know,' I said when it was over, 'that was really very good.'

'Thank you,' she said.

'But,' I said. I paused. What I wanted to say was, if you can play the piano really quite well, not very excitingly but quite well, why do you want to tell lies all the time about stupid things? Isn't that enough for you? But what I really said was, 'That bit about six bars in. A bit slower? Let's try again.'

Three weeks later, I spoke to Heinrich, back from England.

'I've found an accompanist,' I said. 'A good one.'

'Oh yes?' Heinrich said, a little put out. He enjoyed the intimacy of our rehearsals.

'What did you do in England?' I said.

'Well, I saw Lord Harcourt.'

'You just saw him?'

'Well, actually I stayed in his house for a few days. He believed all that stuff about my being a very good friend of Archy's and yours.'

'No reason why he shouldn't, of course,' I said, 'since it's true.'

'Of course,' he said. 'I met the ex-wife, as well.'

'What, Lady Harcourt?' I said, disbelievingly.

'Yes,' he said. 'I couldn't work it out. I think they see quite a lot of her still. Your grandmother was being terribly sweet to her. It was a bit sinister. You were mean about her, by the way. She's really not all that bad.'

'Maybe she isn't,' I said. 'Archy says she's hard-done-by. I just can't stand the way she stands and looks at you, like *that*.'

'Nothing wrong with the way she looks at you,' said Heinrich, not seeing at all.

'All right,' I said. 'I just dislike the fact that she's going to go on calling herself Lady Harcourt long after my grandmother becomes Lady Harcourt.' This hadn't occurred to me before, and didn't worry me now that it had, although I knew it would be exercising my grandmother.

'You really do talk the most incredible nonsense sometimes,' said Heinrich indulgently. 'But, you know, I tried to get your grandmother on to the subject of your grandfather. I just wanted to find out about the music. But she wouldn't talk about it at all. She seemed angry when I said you'd told me about the fact that he'd written music. All she wanted to know is if I'd heard any of his music apart from the violin sonata. I just said, no, no. And then she said, of course, never mind. And she seemed a bit ashamed to have been so rude.'

'Did you ask her about the *Lulu* manuscript?' I said.

'No,' said Heinrich, and in turn looked a little ashamed. 'What does Lord Harcourt think about the whole thing, anyway?'

'No idea,' I said. 'He made all the right noises when the violinist came here to play the sonata, though he kept calling it a concerto, but then he always makes the right noises. I suppose he's just putting up with it, like everyone else.'

'I got on really fairly well with Lady Harcourt, though,' said Heinrich, giving up. 'She seems all right. A bit English, I see that. But she and I went out for the day. She offered to drive me into the countryside. It was really charming, and we went to an English pub in the countryside and had lunch, and we had a very nice chat, and all in all it was one of the nicest days I had all the time I was in England. You know, she said she'd never met you. If you ask me, it sounds as if she's forgotten everything and she's ready to forgive you for everything.'

'Mm-hmm,' I said, fluently.

At this point a year passed.

THIRTY-ONE

During which nothing happened. My grandmother became Lady Harcourt, after a token period when she considered going round preserving the glorious memory of my grandfather by calling herself Lady Weissmann-Harcourt, or Helga Weissmann, Lady Harcourt, or Lady (Helga) Harcourt. In the end she decided that no one could possibly forget that she had been married to my grandfather, or mistake her for the former Lady Harcourt. Which was her other worry.

The other Lady Harcourt was still hanging round Lord Harcourt's house at the time of the wedding. My grandmother had long since given up being nice to her, and taken to attempting to get rid of her from her husband's life, with no success.

Heinrich gave me an account of what Lord Harcourt and his former wife were like together, and according to him, she came round for the afternoon every afternoon, and always stayed for dinner. They never talked very much, the two of them, and she seemed to spend most of her time telling the servants to move furniture around. I would have thought that my grandmother was quite well equipped to deal with this kind of behaviour, but perhaps she had been persuaded to put up with it by Lord Harcourt.

Archy thought that his mother was expecting some kind of role at the wedding. Renunciator, perhaps, or chief weeper. I don't know. She didn't get it, though. The wedding took place in Cambridge, which was a tremendous cause for complaint among all the old ladies who used to come round and put up with my singing, long before. Vociferation in opposition to an English wedding was audible as far away as Vienna. Nevertheless, hardly any of the old ladies went as far as refusing their invitations. Curiosity was too strong, and their lives were too empty.

What I was completely unprepared for, at the wedding, were the clothes. I should have been warned when Archy produced something he called a morning suit and a black top hat, which he showed fairly serious signs of wanting to wear. Only after a week of concentrated ridicule did he give way. He spent another week sulking, and in the end, next to the other guests, he wouldn't have looked too ludicrous. The morning of the wedding, my mother and I went for a walk, and you could see the women coming through the streets, in the hats and veils no sane person would ever put on. Their embarrassed husbands, their special outfits.

Perhaps my grandmother was used to absurdity; certainly, married to Lord Harcourt, she would have no choice but to get used to it. But she outdid even the most vulgar of the English women by appearing in an enormous white wedding dress, and hiring some seven-year-old nephews of Lady Harcourt to carry her train, sulking, up the aisle. The English didn't seem to mind, with the exception of Lady Harcourt, who couldn't even admire her sailor-suited nephews, but the German old ladies, quiet, respectable and sober-suited, seemed numb, as though they had been hit on the back of the head.

Lord Harcourt grinned throughout, and my grandmother wiped away ersatz tears beneath her veil at regular intervals, and a child threw a slice of cake at another child. The tent like a parachute in the garden, the gilt tables, the band and the loud voices and the high colour of the English women, their heels sinking into the lawn.

Heinrich and Archy and I stayed with my grandmother

and Lord Harcourt before the wedding – my grandmother, despite her insistence on the white dress, had a robust lack of self-consciousness about living with her future husband. Heinrich was delighted to be invited to the wedding, and spent most of the time comforting Archy's mother, which no one else would have done.

And that was all until the summer, when my grandmother sent the *Lulu* manuscript back to me, rather than to Archy. And suddenly it was like an intrusion on our easy lives. She said it was very interesting, but she couldn't really say how important it was. I told Archy, but he was still unwilling to talk about it. I would have asked him whether he had asked my grandmother for any more of my grandfather's music, but I don't think I would have got an answer. My grandmother, speaking grand Berlin German to the college servants, was far away in England. I didn't know whether she seemed distant in her letters because she *was* distant, or because of some other reason. The evening when she had told me how she had met my grandfather, we had seemed to have a proper conversation as never really before. Afterwards, nothing had changed, and perhaps her chilliness was just the old manner I had forgotten. Or perhaps it was a new chilliness which set in with the artifice and grandeur of her new wedding, her new husband, her new name.

So I went on as usual. After a soprano walked out at the opera, I was Sophie in *Der Rosenkavalier* at short notice. It had always been one of my grandmother's favourite operas, and it wasn't as if I had to learn the part. I just turned up and skipped girlishly round the stage and, frankly, sang along with the orchestra. It left my brain agreeably disengaged, every night observing the sobbing expensive masses coldly. And the papers were full of the fairy tale of the unknown soprano who saved the day, which Archy and I read to each other until we were sick with laughter.

'Do you like it?' he said.

'I think it's absolutely marvellous,' I said. 'I've never in my whole life ever been moved quite so much by anything at all.'

'Are you serious?' he said.

'No,' I said. 'I was quoting a fan letter.'

'Oh, lucky you,' he said, rather acidly. 'I didn't know you had been singing at benefits for the deaf.'

In the late spring, I started rehearsing for *Lulu*. Oh, how I hated that *Lulu*, its skirls and flourishes, its luxuriance and its shrieks. I hadn't seen Charlotte for a few months, but I telephoned her to ask her to play the piano for me, as I knew that having Archy or Heinrich playing would slow everything down and make it all much more unpleasant.

'Well, I can't,' she said.

'Why not?' I said, annoyed. After all, most people would have thought I was doing her a favour.

'Can I come round?' she said.

'Of course,' I said.

When she came in, I saw immediately why. She was at least six months pregnant.

'How did it happen?' I said, as people always do.

'The usual way,' she said, as people always do.

I wanted to know who the father was, since I had always thought that Charlotte was going to devote her life to her fruitless passion for Archy. If it was him, I wondered if I should do something about it. It seemed terribly unlikely.

Anyway, it seemed quite clear that Charlotte wasn't going to be able to play the piano too strenuously, since in another month or two she wouldn't be able to do the dusting. I would have preferred her to play the piano for me, she was so enjoyable, easy and dull. She never complained, she only lied, and I had long ago forgotten I ever disliked her.

In the end Archy and Heinrich played for me. They thought they were insisting, since I didn't mention Charlotte's pregnancy to either of them. They thought it was the only way I would learn the part. Maybe they were right. They played in turn, like relay runners, until their irritation became a heavy baton to pass on to the other. They would play a phrase, I would sing it back. They corrected a wrong note, or an ugly way of phrasing, and, the music in front of me, I would have another go. My aim was memory, and their aim was patience, and neither one nor the other of us was much good at it.

I felt I would never learn the part; never be able to switch off and just leave the tune and my throat to do the rest. At first we got through a scene a day, or half a scene, stopping and starting as Lulu began to sing and stopped singing. We went through from beginning to end three times, and then we went back and forth, picking up bits and hammering fruitlessly at insoluble problems. And then there came a time when we got through the first act on Monday, and the second act on Tuesday ('Heinrich and I had almost finished the first act when he went,' I said to Archy), and the whole opera on Wednesday, and the whole opera on Thursday. On Friday, Archy said 'Well?' to me, and I thought for a second, and I found I had forgotten everything.

Every word, every note, every phrase. Whenever I started, I couldn't remember what speed to begin at. I didn't know what came next, or why, and I watched the notes on the line, as if they were going to move from me. It was as if something was coming between me and my voice, and it was the music.

It was like . . . it was like nothing, really. A weekend went by, and another week, and until Thursday we didn't try to practise. We didn't decide not to. We just didn't mention it. But on Thursday, Heinrich came round to see if

I'd made any progress. I think he was a little horrified when I said I'd done nothing for a week. After all, time was limited, and difficulties were there to be overcome.

'Do you remember it?' he said.

'No, not at all,' I said.

'Nothing?' he said.

'Nothing,' I said.

He was sceptical. Until the last week, I had been singing it every day for two months. I must remember something. I did remember something. I was just pretending, just temporarily stuck, surely.

'No,' I said.

Heinrich sent Archy away, and we went into the drawing room. He sat down awkwardly at the piano, taking my copy of the music, and began to play. Not from where I came in, but from the beginning of the opera. He played and sang the long prologue while I stood, musicless, and waited. I was patient. I knew I wouldn't be able to sing anything, when he reached the end of the prologue, and listened to his half-speech, half-song with polite interest, as if I were a member of an audience.

Heinrich reached the end of the prologue and began immediately to play the music of the first scene. I thought, I could go. I don't have to stay here. And Heinrich looked up at me, grinning like a devil with his wriggling and his half-music and his lewd power.

'*Jetzt!*' he said.

And then it was all right.

I don't know what it was. I still didn't know the music. But suddenly my voice did. We got to the end of the first act, and, with no pause, went into the second. Heinrich sang in *basso* and *falsetto* and spoke and bellowed, tunes in the orchestra his fingers couldn't tackle, lines of singers, other parts, other people one never thought of. I noted his ugly noises, the approximations and splashes at the piano, and casually heard the gorgeous confidences of my voice, realizing that it, at least, knew how it went.

Something was standing between me and my voice, but it wasn't the music. It was fear, and I watched it evaporate, and, with it, my dislike of *Lulu*, which had only ever been a dislike of what I couldn't do.

'Isn't this,' I sang, 'the divan on which your father bled to death?'

Heinrich, playing his final doomy chords, looked at me quizzically.

'*Verblutet hat!*' I said, '*Verblutet hat!*'

The end of the act was lost. Heinrich stopped and watched my hilarity until it subsided into silent shaking and tears of after-laughter. He watched me until I was silent with giggles.

'*Und jetzt?*' he said. I shook my head. It was long ago dark outside. My voice, altogether elsewhere, just kept laughing and laughing and laughing.

'Do you know about Charlotte?' I said, eventually.

THIRTY-TWO

'What's it like, being pregnant?' I said to Charlotte. A pianist was trying to play some exceptionally nasty part of *Lulu*, and we had to raise our voices to hear each other.

'Well, awful,' she said. 'First you spend weeks and weeks in a state of panic, then you're sick all the time and you want to eat peculiar food, then you get piles, and then you can't go to sleep and your back hurts the whole time, and you feel just incredibly ugly even though everyone keeps telling you how healthy you look.'

'You know,' I said, 'if I couldn't see for myself that you were pregnant, I would have thought you were making it up from books.'

'Well, the odd thing is,' Charlotte said, 'that being pregnant is just like it says in the books. I wanted to be original, but everybody is pregnant in exactly the same way, in the end, unless your baby's born blue or something.'

'Who's the father?' I said.

'Not Archy,' she said promptly.

'You shock me,' I said languidly. 'I wish he'd stop doing that.'

'It is disagreeable,' Charlotte said.

The soprano engaged for Lulu had decided that the run was too long and the performances too close together. So, after what Heinrich described as a lengthy series of discussions attended by solicitors, during which she attempted to diminish her work as much as possible without diminishing her fee, she agreed to perform at five performances. I had two in between, rather than just sitting round as a fruitless and eager understudy.

This meant that, rather than just learning the part at home, or at Heinrich's, I had to go to all the rehearsals. Charlotte often came with me. Most of the time I sat and read my cook book, which for some reason made everyone worry that I was pregnant as well and would be no good for Lulu. The performances were only of the first two acts, of course. The third act would be left out, and, instead, two ten-minute stretches which were already known, would be played by the orchestra. Apparently these came from yet another version of *Lulu*, an orchestral version.

'My god,' I said to Archy when Charlotte and I got home from the rehearsal, 'is there no end to these *Lulu*s? These other *Lulu*s?'

'No,' said Archy. 'There might be another one, somewhere, another secret version, another orchestral version, a quadrille for piano duet, a fantasy for string sextet on themes from *Lulu*. Who knows? It's alive.'

'Hatching,' I said. 'But why not the third act? It's here. It could be done. You haven't stolen it. What's the objection?'

'One day,' said Archy. 'I don't know when. Do you want some tea, Charlotte?'

Charlotte was in the drawing room. I think she enjoyed sitting in a warm flat on a comfortable sofa, and Archy, awed by her fecundity, had stopped being rude to her, and was even offering her cups of tea without being prompted.

'No thanks,' she said. In fact, what Charlotte seemed to like was cheese, as Archy would have known if he had been in the habit of looking in the cupboard.

'I'll have one,' I said. He looked at me, as if to suggest that I could make it myself, and started kicking the table disconsolately.

In fact, when rehearsals started with the orchestra, I

was fairly glad that only two acts were involved. It was a real killer, full of coloratura and bellowing over the din in the pit and fancy stuff, and, in this production, lots of jumping around and tightrope walking and swinging from the lights. It took me a long time to grasp the plot, since there were so many men, and they were all more or less the same, but it went something like this. Lulu is married to a doctor who bursts down the door one day while she's having her portrait painted and dies of a heart attack. The painter marries her and is persuaded to commit suicide by an old lover of Lulu's. The old lover is shot by Lulu just before she marries him, and she goes to prison. She escapes with the help of an old Lesbian countess who she possibly has an affair with, and has an affair with the old lover's son. All through, she's pursued by a Prince, an Athlete, a Schoolboy, an Asthmatic, and so on. In the third act, Archy told me, she's pursued by a Marquis, a Negro and Jack the Ripper, who finally kills her. The Lesbian is called Geschwitz, the Old Lover Doctor Schön, the Old Lover's Son Alwa and the Asthmatic Schigolch. Everyone else is just called after their job, except Lulu. It was terribly confusing.

'What's the point of it?' I asked Archy and Heinrich.

They both said the same thing. They said, 'The music.'

They had a point. What had seemed harsh and unappealing in Archy's flat, played badly by Archy and Heinrich was, played by the orchestra, gorgeous and floating. I relished the pantomime transformation, and waited for my own. There was something almost delicious, almost edible about the velvety near-operetta sound about me, a glittering heartless chaste excess of means to achieve the utterly limpid, the virtually unsingable, irresistibly hummable musics. I knew that I couldn't, but always at the end of the second act, I wanted to go on. Heinrich was conducting, and I used to say this to him, and he used to say, 'Of course. You've seen the third act.' I liked to go on teasing him with it. It was too difficult to flirt with him. It led too quickly to a conclusion of some sort. I was practising the part, to Archy's irritation, from his manuscript. And holding it up to Heinrich as a temptation, which might in the end lead to some of my grandfather's music, could go on endlessly. This was useful, since so did the rehearsals.

'I don't know why you put up with it,' Charlotte said. I had a cup of tea and had brought her a lump of cheese, which from time to time she gnawed at with polite curiosity. 'It's not as if you enjoy singing, or anything.'

'No,' I said.

'Or want to be famous,' she said, as if she were asking a question.

'No,' I said, more tentatively.

'Or like music,' she said.

'I like some music,' I said.

'You don't like this,' she said.

'Not like, exactly,' I said. 'I think it's quite impressive, and I like having sung it, if you see what I mean.'

'But not singing it,' she said.

'Not really,' I said. 'But I've got to do it now. And it won't go on for ever.'

'It might,' she said.

THIRTY-THREE

Archy's flat had always had a life of its own, filling up with so many books and papers and music and carpets that it seemed a living thing. Archy thought so too, I think, and often remarked in a complacent way that the flat was looking terrible, as if it were a maiden aunt suffering from some growth which would eventually kill it. Once, I came home and found a small harpsichord nestling in the crook of the grand piano. 'Oh, I bought it,' Archy would always say of these acquisitions, as if there were any question about it.

But for some reason it was at this period that I decided that the moment had come to do something about it. I knew that there was no point in throwing anything out. So I had a carpenter come, and in the place of the three quite inadequate bookshelves which stood in the drawing room, he built shelves around the entire drawing room. It took two days, and another day to put what one could on the shelves, and at the end of it, every terrible novel and every scrap of music and every record which had been lying on the floor was on a shelf, in alphabetical order, and could be found, and there was nothing on the floor except eleven Persian carpets, one on top of the other. The room was smaller by about a foot and a half in every direction, but that was trivial.

The order that had come to the flat didn't last, and I knew at the time that it wouldn't. Archy seemed to think that this was a permanent order, and said nothing about the shelves, or the order, or the carpenter. And now I think of it, it seems to me that those three days marked the end of my marriage. In those three days, Charlotte sat contentedly in the kitchen, and the carpenter banged and sang in the drawing room, and Archy and I walked about the flat, performing a small pavane of polite giving way around each other when we met in the hallway or coming out of the bedroom. Archy had never been polite, and his politeness was like an embodiment of fear.

And after three days, the carpenter had gone, and Charlotte hadn't yet arrived, and we were alone in the strange flat with each other.

'Do you like music?' I said to Archy.

'What kind of question is that?'

'A real one,' I said.

'Of course I do,' he said.

'Do you like *Lulu*?' I said.

'Yes, more than anything,' he said.

'What are you going to do with the manuscript?' I said.

'Nothing,' he said.

'You have to do something,' I said.

'No, not necessarily,' he said.

'Too many people know about it,' I said. 'They all want to know if it just disappeared, or if you just sat on it.'

'So,' he said, after a while of thinking, 'who knows about it?'

'You. Me. My grandmother. And I told Heinrich about it.'

'Oh Christ.'

'I'm afraid so.'

'My father?'

'I suppose so. Is he coming, by the way?'

'I suppose so. Your grandmother certainly is. My mother said she would.'

'Your mother?'

'Yes. Why not?'

'No reason,' I said.

Every day I followed Archy round the flat, picking up the books he had begun to read, and the records he had begun to play, and placed them on the shelves in a proper order. It was only not caring about him, and feeling quite indifferent to his wants and his needs that made me able to clear up after him, as if he were a boy who couldn't help it. I cooked and cleaned, and I didn't resent it, and I didn't like it. And from time to time we were in the same room or the same bed, and embarked on neutral politeness, or hostile discussions of music.

'What,' I said, 'does my grandmother really think about this manuscript?'

'No idea,' he said.

'You must know.'

'No,' said Archy. 'I've really no idea. How should I know?'

'Hasn't she written you about my grandfather's music?'

'No. Nothing more. The violin sonata, and that's it.'

'Have you asked her for some more?'

'Well, yes, I have.'

'And?'

'And nothing. No reply at all.'

'When was this?'

'Just after their wedding, I think.'

'Honestly, do you think there might be something in all this music?'

'I don't know. I take your grandmother's word for it.'

'No,' I said. 'That's not really what I meant. I meant, do you think my grandfather's music is actually any good, from what you've seen?'

'Yes,' said Archy. 'Yes, I do.'

'You do?' I said. 'Isn't that wonderful?'

There was a little silence, and Archy looked down at his hands, looking for a second completely unhappy and lost and bemused.

'And you've no idea,' I went on, 'what she thinks about the *Lulu* manuscript, you don't know if she thinks it's about her, or anything?'

'I don't think it's about anyone,' said Archy.

'It must be about someone,' I said.

'I don't think Berg actually slept with this Luise, you know. Even if she existed. Which she didn't.'

'Why do you think that?'

'Well, I actually know it,' said Archy.

'How do you know it?' I said.

'I just do,' said Archy.

'How can you know something like that?' I said.

'Well,' said Archy.

'Where is this manuscript from?' I said.

'Well,' said Archy.

'Archy,' I said, making a great leap of thought and not stopping to breathe, 'is this manuscript real?'

'Real?'

'Real.'

'What do you mean?'

'Is it by Berg?'

'The music?'

'No.'

'The journal?'

'Yes.'

'Oh no,' said Archy, peeling a banana and offering me half. 'Of course not.'

'I don't believe you like music at all,' I said, refusing the banana, for obvious reasons.

THIRTY-FOUR

'I don't believe you,' I said, for what seemed like the fortieth time. We were lying in bed. At least I was. Archy was sitting on the side of the bed, eating his banana. What I said didn't disturb me, and I felt that it should. I said it again.

'I don't believe you,' I said.

'What don't you believe?' said Archy.

'Everything,' I said. 'Where did you get it from, if it's not real?'

'Frau Egon gave it to me,' said Archy.

'No, she didn't,' I said. 'Don't lie to me. Where does it really come from?'

'Why don't you believe me?'

'I don't believe you,' I said, not seeing quite why I was going on with this.

'What do I have to do?' said Archy. 'Why won't you believe me? I am your husband, you know.'

I looked at him without changing my expression. 'I won't believe you because what you're telling me isn't true.' Archy finished eating his banana, concentrating, a little frown. He held up the banana's skin, had no pocket to put it in, dropped it on the floor. Then he said,

'You're right.'

The telephone rang. We looked at it for a while before I picked it up. It was Charlotte, of course, asking if she could come round for the afternoon. I refused, for once. There was a brief silence at the other end, and it's true that people don't often refuse pregnant women things.

'That was Charlotte,' I said.

'Charlotte?' Archy said. 'Oh yes. Do you know who the father of the baby is?'

'I rather thought it was you,' I said unblinkingly.

'Me?' said Archy with genuine surprise.

'Yes,' I said. 'So. Where does the *Lulu* manuscript come from?'

'I wrote it,' said Archy, then, theatrically, he clapped his hand over his mouth. I looked long and hard at him for any of the signs of lying, but I couldn't see a single one, and I wondered if he could possibly be telling me the truth.

That was a long afternoon. We lay in bed, and Archy seemed unable to stop telling me things. He kept saying he was telling me everything, and perhaps he was. And perhaps he wasn't telling me lies. It wasn't until the very end of the afternoon that I realized that he wasn't lying, I had got so much into the habit of disbelieving him. But I think now it was probably all true.

The manuscript, which I had told Heinrich was the most real thing I had ever seen, had been concocted by Archy on a stash of old music paper out of a printed score of *Lulu*, a piano score of the third act which was out of the hands of the widow and well known, although not by me, and a goodish knowledge of Berg's style and a knack of imitating handwriting.

'Think about it,' said Archy. 'Who's seen it?'

'I have,' I said. 'And my grandmother. And Heinrich.'

'Quite,' Archy said. 'And you and your grandmother aren't in a position to tell the difference, anyway. And Heinrich, you said.'

'And Heinrich?' I said.

'Nothing,' Archy said. 'So none of you know much about Berg, clearly. You were easily impressed.'

I said Heinrich had seen it without thinking, though he only knew about it. But it was surprising that Archy took the information without challenging it, for, after all, if Heinrich had seen it, it could only have been through me.

'But now,' Archy said, 'it's of no importance. I wish I'd never done it.'

'Why?' I said.

'Because something much more important and interesting's come up,' he said.

'My grandfather's music, you mean?' I said.

'Yes,' he said.

'But what's that got to do with you?' I said. I meant it. It was my grandfather's music first, and then it was my grandmother's, with her romantic tale of their elopement and their marriage and their money. And then it was nobody's, and certainly not Archy's.

Archy took a moment to understand quite what I meant. 'It's to do with me because none of you understand that this might be something really worthwhile, a real find. Somebody's got to do something with it, get it played, for goodness' sake.'

'Why you?'

'Because I happened to be there,' he said. 'Don't be so ridiculous.'

'What's all this got to do with the *Lulu* manuscript?'

'Nothing, of course. Or it had nothing until you sent the stupid thing to your grandmother. And before that she was keen to get all her husband's music to me, because of what I did for the violin sonata. I know you don't appreciate these things, but the violin sonata's a really impressive piece of work.'

'Well, why hasn't she sent you some more?'

'I don't know,' Archy said. 'But since she saw the manuscript, she's been completely different. She used to phone me, you know, and write and stuff. I asked her for some more stuff from her cupboards, as I said. And she just hasn't replied. I think she must have found someone else who's interested in the music.'

'It doesn't seem very likely,' I said.

'I think there might be something in the journal I put into the manuscript,' Archy said reflectively. 'I can't think what.'

'Why did you put it in?' I said.

'What, the journal?' Archy said. 'I can't really remember. It is the sort of thing Berg used to do, or might be quite likely to do. And I suppose I thought it would make it a bit more difficult to compare it with the real *Lulu*, and a bit more interesting. But I think something in it's upset your grandmother, or made her not want to deal with someone who knows anything about it. It's all about some mistress of Berg's. Maybe she had an affair with him.'

'Unimaginable,' I said. 'Why did it have to be a pupil of Berg's, anyway?'

'Sheer bad luck,' Archy said. 'It could have been anyone, but what I thought of was a pupil. He did have pupils, after all.'

'And my grandfather was one of them,' I said. 'Can I ask you one thing?'

'Of course,' said Archy.

'Why did you do it?'

'What, write the manuscript?' he said.

'Yes,' I said.

'Gaiety of nations,' said Archy without pause.

'What?' I said.

'I thought it would add to the gaiety of nations.'

'What on earth do you mean?'

'I originally planned to write this thing, and let all the musicologists write admiring articles in all the papers about it. And then, after a year or two, I'd reveal that I wrote it, and they'd look ridiculous, and it would add immeasurably to the gaiety of nations.'

He looked, at that moment, utterly small and ridiculous and wretched. I just looked at him. He started to get dressed so that he wouldn't have to look at me.

'And now,' I said, 'you'd do absolutely anything not to have written it, wouldn't you? Because you've no idea whatsoever what my grandmother is doing with all that music, and who she's going to give it to.'

Archy stood in his shirt, barefoot, and looked with great intensity at the ground, and said, 'Yes.'

'What?' I said.

'I said Yes,' said Archy. 'That's absolutely true.'

Trouserless, Archy created an unexpected belief around him, evacuated the space of questioning. Then he stepped forward and fell on the banana skin. I had to leave it.

THIRTY-FIVE

Archy was still nursing his knee when the telephone began to ring. I left him and went into his drawing room to answer it.

'Friederike,' said Charlotte.

'Charlotte,' I said.

'Are you busy?' she said.

'No,' I said.

'Can I come round this evening?' she said.

'Yes, all right,' I said. I didn't think for a second who I was talking to, or consider whether I actually wanted Charlotte to come round, as I knew what the answer would be. I didn't want to see anyone, even Charlotte. It was unnatural that I didn't think, 'Even Archy,' but what I thought was, 'Even Charlotte.' I put the telephone down on her effusive thanks, and decided to go out immediately.

I looked at the flat in the way I never had to. So many books of his, so few of mine. I had hardly changed his life, had hardly anything left of mine. Rewritten, my life was saturated with his, his barely tainted with mine. I had brought nothing to his life except shelves. I ran my hand along one, from *Trust* to *Rage* to *Jealousy* to *Destiny*. Blunt, empty, titles, giving nothing away, waiting for a reader, waiting for Archy.

But our lives were about to change, I knew it. If I had reached the point where my life was utterly emptied, I knew that at any moment I was going to turn about and recapture not just my life, but Archy's as well, and, outside the slammed door to the flat, I hugged myself a little.

Archy had given me an explanation. I almost believed

it. I almost wanted to believe it. The one thing wrong with it was that it didn't explain anything at all. But now I had it, I couldn't pursue the subject and we both knew it.

He used to say, my husband, that music didn't mean anything, that it just was. I don't know about this. I suppose it doesn't mean anything very accurate in the end. But it certainly seems to mean things to people, and I don't know if that's something different. And if it didn't mean anything at all, then it couldn't tell the truth, and it couldn't lie. But what was *Lulu*? An enormous lie, and what was my grandfather's piece? Something novelettishly real and true and sincere. For me, though I couldn't really say whether it was inventive, or original, or dynamic, or any of those things, it told me the truth, whatever the truth might be. And, when I came back from the succession of bars I had been sitting in, I put on the recording of the violin sonata, too loud for the neighbours at an hour between midnight and dawn, and began, maybe for the first time, to listen to it. And Archy came out in his pyjamas rubbing his eyes and yawning like a husband in a cartoon and looked at me in my fur coat and my glass of whisky, and I looked back levelly at him.

That year, that empty year, out of which the two acts of *Lulu* had begun to emerge cleanly like a broken bridge, began to fill with thought and Berg and the exotic truths of conspiracy. Now we both thought Heinrich had seen the manuscript, there was no point in my not handing it over. After a little unwillingness, he agreed to look at it. I told him flatly that Archy had some doubt about its authenticity, and chose an afternoon when I was supposed to be practising *Lulu*, to give us a chance to be alone.

Heinrich didn't laugh at it, and he looked at it from the beginning. He turned the pages a little too carefully, touching only their edges with the back of his hand, breathing out of the side of his mouth. I watched him, but only occasionally did he look, full of worry and concern, as if reminded of something, at me.

'What do you think?' I said at the end.

There was a very long pause indeed.

'Friederike,' Heinrich said. 'I have to tell you that I've actually seen this before. About two years ago.'

'You've seen it before?'

'Yes,' Heinrich said. 'Archy showed it to me.'

'I see,' I said. 'And what do you think?'

'I think now what I thought then,' he said. 'Which is that it's a feeble forgery perpetrated and probably carried out by Archy.'

'I see,' I said, making a good performance of somebody coping well with disastrous news.

'I'm sorry to say this,' Heinrich said. 'But it wouldn't fool anyone who knew anything about Berg for ten minutes.'

'It fooled me,' I said. Heinrich kindly didn't bother to respond to this. 'But why did he do anything so absurd?'

'Well,' Heinrich said. 'I don't really want to say.'

'No, go on,' I said. 'After all, I ought to know the worst.'

'Well,' Heinrich said. 'I think he just wants to be famous and great. I think it's just a hunger for glory. Imagine, you know, being the person who discovered the complete manuscript of Berg's *Lulu*. Or the person who successfully fooled a lot of musicologists with a brilliantly executed forgery. It would be almost as good as writing Berg's *Lulu* yourself. Think of that.'

'Though not,' I said, 'quite as good as discovering and editing the complete works of a completely unheard-of genius.'

'Quite,' said Heinrich. 'But what happened was that he picked on me to show the score to, after he'd left it in the rain for a while. I saw straight away what it was, and told him that he'd be wise to forget all about it and throw it away, if he wanted to keep his job and what reputation he had. Which I thought he'd done, until you started telling me about this very interesting score of *Lulu* your husband had discovered. I hate to say it, but he uses it to impress people who don't know any better.'

'Like his wife,' I said.

'Like his wife,' Heinrich said. 'Now let's go to bed.'

Archy's tinsel glory got into my Lulu, and I rode the edge of the orchestra pit, looking down at Heinrich, perspiring, and sang, my voice full of a contempt no one heard and no one would have thought was directed at them. Heinrich would smile back at me, encouragingly, and I knew he was thinking that my improvement, the effortless beauty of tone and the cold and beguiling accuracy were due to the resumption of our affair. There hadn't seemed a lot of point in not carrying on with it.

I knew he thought my improvement was due to him because he told me. I didn't believe in the effortless beauty of my tone, nor in the cold and beguiling accuracy, and I thought he was telling me these things for reasons of his own. I did believe, just as I had believed before, that he was right to say that any improvement was due to my having an affair with him. He was right because only after that did I begin to despise him for what he had told me, and only after that did I find the right noises for Lulu.

Every day now we would practise a terrifying moment, dreamt up by the producer and refused by the diva. I didn't have the confidence or the security to be able to refuse anything the producer wanted me to do, so I did it. The moment came just before Lulu shot Doctor Schön. He forced her to her knees to beg forgiveness. Why, I never found out. A heavy chandelier was hanging from the flies directly above, a stage oak table below that. At this point,

Lulu leapt up, pushing Doctor Schön aside, jumped on to the table and with a single bound was hanging from the chandelier. From which point, swinging to and fro, she sang her long aria telling Doctor Schön and the wedding party what she wanted in life. This was the idea, anyway.

In reality, the Doctor Schön always got carried away with his brutality and started, halfway through rehearsals, kneeling on the back of my neck, then putting me into a half-nelson. He always made me struggle to get loose. I needed more time to get through these leaps and bounds, more time to collect myself and think of the next notes than he ever gave me, and I lived in fear that one night I would find myself beginning the aria with a strained muscle or a broken arm. Once clear of the psychopathic baritone, leaping on to the table needed a great amount of faith and fearlessness. The leap, invented by the producer as rehearsals progressed, had not been taken into account by whoever thought up and built the table, which, though it looked solid, was as wobbly and tacked-together as most stage furniture. The bang of my landing was always followed by a slow creak from the table, which one day I knew would collapse as I was standing on it. And once hanging from the chandelier, I was lucky if I could produce any noises with my arms stretched painfully upwards, swinging to and fro pushed by eager stage hands, and luckier still if I could remember how it went. It was the moment in the opera which in Berg's secret journal, or Archy's forged journal, the original words were left unchanged. For some reason this made the whole thing much more difficult to remember.

I was hanging from the chandelier one day and had just sung *Wenn sich die Menschen um meinetwillen* and only that, when Heinrich stopped the orchestra.

'Late,' he said.

'I'm sorry,' I said, still hanging from the chandelier.

'It's always late,' he said.

'You know,' I said, 'I need more time, I really do. It's terribly difficult to sing like this. I don't think you appreciate the problems you're imposing on me.'

The orchestra started giggling like a lot of girls. 'Start earlier,' said Heinrich, smiling. He knew that I had terrible trouble with the enthusiastic baritone, and had turned it into a kind of joke with me.

'Couldn't you wait a moment to see if I'm there yet?' I said, forlornly.

'Well, not really,' said Heinrich. 'Not without completely losing what impetus we're managing to create. And the wonderful luscious sound from the strings.'

He was often offensively sycophantic towards the orchestra in rehearsals. 'All right,' I said, still hanging from the chandelier.

'No, no,' said Heinrich, 'from the kneeling bit.' He never knew the words or, really, what was going on.

I dropped painfully from the chandelier on to the table, and lay there sprawled for a moment. It all seemed like a tremendous amount of trouble and pain for a lot of people I disliked.

'Couldn't I simply jump on to the table and sing it?' I said, dusting myself off hopelessly.

Heinrich turned round to the darkened auditorium where the producer was in deep conversation with the director of the opera house, who had just dropped in to see how things were going.

'What?' said the producer.

'Couldn't she just sing the aria from the top of a table?' said Heinrich.

The producer raised his nose in the air and sniffed, as though thinking deeply. Then he said, 'No, not really,' and carried on talking to the director of the house. The producer, in five weeks of rehearsals, never managed to remember Heinrich's name, or my name, or, now I come to think of it, Berg's name. But he was very keen on acrobatics and pouting and generally behaving in a mysterious and irresistible manner, which, naturally, I was terribly good at.

'All right,' I said. The music began its familiar clamour, and I turned to the Doctor Schön, lumbering towards me, his arms carrying invisible suitcases in his idea of brutish uncontrollable rage. In turn, I raised my hands to my mouth in my idea of uncontrollable panic.

'If for my sake a man killed himself or others, my value would still remain what it was. You know the reasons why you wanted to be my husband, and I know my reasons for hoping we should be married. You let your dearest friends be cheated by what you made me do,' I sang, in the theatre.

'Yet you can't consider yourself caught in your own deception. From me you've had my youth in flower. I have not asked in my life to appear in another colour than the one which I am known to have,' I sang, at home, 'nor has any man in my life been led to look on me as other than what I am.'

'Yes,' said Archy, at home. He paused and looked at me. I was panting a little. 'Keep hold of the line.'

'What do you mean?' I said.

'Just think of the direction of the whole aria,' Archy said. I knew he was saying this because he couldn't think of anything else to say, since it didn't mean anything at all.

'All right,' I said. 'I'll try.'

'Again,' said Archy. 'Here we go.'

'*Wenn sich die Menschen um meinetwillen*,' I sang.

'Now on the floor,' said Archy.

'If for my sake,' I sang. No trouble.

'Now with your arms above your head,' said Archy.

'*Wenn sich um meinetwillen*,' I sang.

'Now hanging from the doorframe,' said Archy. 'Where did you go the other night?'

‘If,’ I sang. ‘I can’t do it,’ I said. ‘I just went out.’

‘I know. Good,’ said Archy. ‘It’s not just bad any more. It’s noticeably worse, anyway.’

‘I know,’ I said. ‘There’s nothing I can do about it.’

‘Probably no one will be listening at this point anyway,’ said Archy. ‘They’ll all be worrying too much about whether you’re actually going to be able to sing the whole aria in this ridiculous position, or whether you’re going to drop off halfway through. Who’s the producer?’

‘A lunatic,’ I said. ‘*Wenn sich die Menschen*,’ I sang. ‘I quite like this bit, actually.’

‘I’m delighted to hear it,’ Archy said. ‘It makes all the difference in the world. Enough.’

THIRTY-SIX

Now they all came, descending from the sky like gods. My mother, and Lady Harcourt, and Frau Egon, and Lord Harcourt, and my grandmother came, and I had made only one plan. The plan was for the food. On the first day Lady Harcourt only was there, and she had soft, white, loving things, meringues and minced chicken and parsnip *veluta*. The next day Frau Egon and my mother and Charlotte came, and, like a taint of blood, a line of pink and of red ran through the dinner, white ravioli in cream filled with tomatoes, pork cooked in milk and threaded with red peppers, *panna cotta* with a sauce of raspberries. On the third day Lord Harcourt and my grandmother came, and the dinner was red and green, two sorts of peppers in oil, baked tomatoes in parsley and garlic, mullet with lentils, and gooseberries and strawberries done into two soufflés. On the fourth day my mother and Heinrich and Lady Harcourt and Archy and Frau Egon and Lord Harcourt and my grandmother and Charlotte sat around the table with one empty seat, and there was yellow and black food, melon soup with caviar, beef in *teriyake* and seared, egg pasta cooked with squid ink and pineapple terrine buried in burnt-black bananas, and cheese for Charlotte, and Lady Harcourt, trained like a seal, ate it all. I put the dishes down with their bright loads and sat in the one empty seat, and they ate, and they went, and on the fifth day, there was *Lulu*.

And standing in front of me, there was my grandmother.

'We ought to talk,' she said.

'Of course,' I said.

'There's something I need to tell you,' she said. 'Let's go for a walk.'

'I need to be back by lunchtime,' I said. I had to dress, and rest before getting to the opera house for three.

'There's no problem,' she said. 'Would you like to go to the art gallery?'

It was so unusual for my grandmother to ask whether I would like to go anywhere, or do anything rather than just do it, and assume that I would fit in with her plans, that I agreed. We left the flat without telling anyone, and took a taxi to the gallery.

'I've never been here before,' my grandmother said, taking my hand.

'It's very good,' I said. 'I came here once when I was fed up, and it cheered me up.'

'Do you remember we used to go to the Dahlem museum together, that month you stayed with us?' she said.

'It was longer than that,' I said. 'Six months, surely.'

'Maybe,' she said. 'You used to hate it, didn't you?'

'No,' I said. 'Not hate it. Not really.'

'Help me up the stairs,' she said, and we hoiked each other up the enormous marble staircase. 'I know that painting.'

'Yes, so do I,' I said. 'What is it?'

'I haven't the faintest idea,' she said with a little asperity. 'It's better not to know, anyway.'

'Archy always wants to know what things are before he knows whether he likes it or not,' I said. 'I don't see the point of it.'

'Perhaps you're right,' she said. 'Sometimes it's better not to know where these things come from.'

We walked for a while through the marble halls. My grandmother was slower than she had been, and no longer trusted to her shooting stick. So we sat down on the benches in the middle of each room, and as we walked, and sat, and stood, and walked, she told me what she wanted to tell me. She often wanted to tell me stories about herself; but all the other stories she had told me many times before. Every other story, it seemed to me, had never been a new story; they had been whispered to me for the first time before I could understand; and when I heard them with understanding for the first time, I already knew how they went. But the story my grandmother told me that day, which she began in the morning in the art gallery, and finished many, many hours later as the grey Vienna dawn was beginning outside the flat, she had never told me before. She never told me the story before, and, because she didn't have to, she never told me it again.

My grandmother, when she was a girl, spent a lot of time going to parties and dinners in Berlin. She went with her husband, a fine young man. He was immensely rich, intelligent, charming, a fine young man, a brilliant musician. She was the estranged daughter of an ordinary middle-class family. They had the glamour of romance; they were not tainted by the old Prussian aristocracy; there was a whiff of scandal about their marriage; there was something new about them, and they were welcomed everywhere.

Many of their friends were artists, composers and writers, among whom they went like foreigners in a country they knew well and spoke the language adequately. Among them was a tall aristocratic, rather frail man, with an odd trick of tipping his head back when he spoke. This man was treated with a great deal of respect even by his close friends. My grandmother first noticed him together with his wife, who was widely considered to be rather unworthy of her husband. Whether you felt sympathy for her or for him, it didn't seem a happy marriage. My grandmother felt sorry for the wife. Then she began to look at the husband, saw how dull most people would seem next to him. Their names were Alban and Helene Berg.

My grandfather was in great awe of Berg, though he was never much afraid of anyone else. He could hardly speak more than the complete minimum necessary to two people who often ate together and moved in the same circle of friends and acquaintances. My grandmother and Berg never spoke to each other, until, one day, they found themselves in the same café, both alone. Alban raised his hat to her. They sat together. She remembered that, at that time, she didn't know whether he was a writer or a composer. He knew very well who she was, which for some reason surprised her. She remembered the delightful, self-deprecating way he hid his surprise at her blunders, her philistinism, and that they sat together all afternoon. At that time, Alban was writing *Lulu*.

'Have you seen my husband's compositions?' she said to him. 'You know, he too is a composer.' 'I should be delighted to, Frau Weissmann,' he said, 'but I should do it only for you.' She was angry with him, and did not mention it to her husband. Then, a week later, when Berg called unannounced on them, to see his work, her husband was angry with her. 'Was there a time when he lost his temper?' I hear my grandmother asking, rhetorically, at his funeral. But maybe she was right. It didn't last. Berg was amused, then impressed. He never took pupils, hardly ever; he took my grandfather.

Sex was what he was writing about, and he looked at her; and what she was feeling, what she never said to anyone until she said it to me, was something she had never felt before, and never since, an overwhelming physical attraction like a new absence inside her.

Like hounds, people sniff desire, and Berg watched her when they were alone, or with my head-down, blinkered, good grandfather, or, once or twice, with Helene Berg, too.

Berg watched her, and she looked at him, when she could. When she thought of him with her husband, what she felt for him was like love; what she felt for her husband was like politeness. Once, when Alban and Helga were alone together, he said, 'You mean a lot to me.' But she didn't trust herself to reply, and smoothing his hair down, he smoothly said, 'Both of you.' She tipped her head back and looked at him. It was a gesture she had picked up from him.

My grandfather saw nothing, or perhaps saw everything. Other things were more important, were more interesting. Liberated by Berg's teaching, he began to compose fluently, began to write and write. Suddenly, he knew how to do it, how the music inside his head went. Next to this, love didn't seem to matter, and the tender politeness with which he and Helga talked to each other when they were alone seemed better than lust, seemed like ordinary goodness, ordinary happiness. And he could not stop writing down the music in his head.

'Put the pieces on one side,' Berg said. Worried by the fluency, the abrupt genius he saw, Berg thought the pieces should be forgotten about, just for a while. He should wait until the meaning of every chord was clear. And then, he should let them go; but once the pieces have been performed, Berg said, they are no longer yours. They are no longer anyone's. Remember that. You think of them as your children, or perhaps your lovers. But remember, it's not just your children who grow up and leave you. The time comes, too, for your lovers to grow up and leave you, and the time comes for your music to grow up, and become unfaithful to you, to leave you. You can't stop it.

And then, after no more than three years' teaching, Berg died, of an absurd, unnecessary infection, leaving an unfinished opera and a young widow. My grandfather never talked about Berg's death to me, and, though my grandmother gave a different impression, he never really talked about it to her. She said he was distraught. He stopped composing, devoted all his time to his wife and daughter, forgot about music, forgot about Berg. It wasn't until 1940 that music began to occur to him again. Returning to what he had written in the three years Berg had taught him, he began to see the merit in it. He began, too, to hear the Berg in his music. The pieces could not be performed, not in Berlin in 1940. So he put them on one side to wait for the end of the war. And slowly, carefully, remembering what Berg had told him about the differences between heard and unheard symphonies, he began to write again. Performance seemed less important. The pieces were his, and they were Helga's, they were my grandmother's. That was enough.

The daughter grew, and my grandfather, abandoned by new music, played Schumann happily in a flat fewer and fewer people visited. Helga grew stout, stopped worrying, grew happy. After all, nothing had happened. And all the time, like mushrooms in the dark, music was growing from my grandfather, writing for himself, not knowing what new music was like, learning about his friends from the obituary pages. A piano concerto, a septet, a triple concerto, an opera on Horváth's *Figaro Gets Divorced* and a song cycle called *Sonnets to Orpheus*. All written in the flat, placed in a drawer, kept from the concert halls, from his friends, from his family, waiting for something. Their friends were ordinary, were not aesthetes, or intellectuals, were happy. Music and Berg were not mentioned, because music was always right, and Berg was wrong. You could, after all, stop music from growing up, from leaving you. Easy.

My grandmother was the guardian of her husband's music. The manuscripts, when he died, were all hers, though the money was all mine. She worried a bit about them, and together with her best friend, she began to write to famous people to ask them to perform some of the pieces. And she wrote to her granddaughter's husband.

She learnt that a manuscript of Berg's great opera was in Archy's possession. She asked to see it, but there seemed to be some difficulties, and it didn't matter. Archy asked to see some of my grandfather's music. A violin sonata was sent with her best friend. Performed, it filled her days with happiness. It was as if she could again hear his speech inflections, his walking rhythms, the peculiar music of his silent smile.

Without warning, her granddaughter gave her the manuscript of *Lulu*. She took it back to Berlin and sent her maid and Lord Harcourt out for the afternoon. She picked it up and began to look at it, not expecting it to mean much to her. It looked like one of Berg's manuscripts. What would she know? It meant something, and she continued to read.

Two hours later, she had to put it down, her arm stiff with rage and thought and rheumatism. She could not destroy it. It was not hers. But, as she listened to her husband's beautiful violin sonata, its complicated happiness seemed to her to be infected with the secret plans and secret lusts of Berg. Why did he teach her husband? To be near her? She could no longer listen to the violin sonata, and innocent, civil references to Berg's music in it seemed like poison. Remarried, her life was poisoned by what she had done without knowing it. His life was poisoned by Berg's without his knowing what the poison meant.

'You see what you did,' she said. 'You needn't say anything. There's nothing you can say.'

I couldn't say anything. I couldn't say that her life had been ruined by a forgery; she would think I was lying to please her. I had, somehow, to prove it to her. But it could never be proved, and that was the end of it.

'That's a wonderful painting,' she said. 'We haven't really been concentrating, have we? But perhaps we ought to go back home.'

'Yes,' I said. It was nearly lunchtime. She held my hand in the taxi, and I knew that she had nothing of recrimination in her, nothing but misery.

'Where did you go?' my mother said, when we got back.

'To the art gallery,' I said. 'It was nice.'

'It's time to go,' she said.

'Maybe,' I said.

'Be good, won't you,' she said, as she used to when I was a child.

'I'll try to,' I said, smiling back.

'Can I do anything?' she said.

'No,' I said, 'not really. I need a lift, though.'

'Good,' she said, 'I'd like to do that, if I may.'

'If you don't mind,' I said. 'The opera house would send someone, if I asked.'

'There's no need,' she said. 'Really. I can drive you, can't I?'

'Of course you can,' I said. If anyone else had said it, I would have wondered if they wanted to tell me something in the car, or if they wanted to get something out of me which meant we would have to be alone. Because it was my mother, I knew that she just wanted to drive me to the opera house, and I was pleased because of it. My mother doesn't come up much in this story, and maybe it's because I always took her sensible clothes and her lack of plotting for granted.

'Am I going to enjoy it?' she said, in the car.

'I hope so,' I said. 'I don't know, though.'

'Is it like your grandfather's piece?' she said.

'Not much,' I said. 'I suppose maybe it is.'

'Oh well,' she said. 'I'm sure it will be just fine. Do you need to know the plot before you go?'

'No,' I said. 'It's too complicated to remember, anyway. Ask Archy if you think you ought to.'

'I don't think I will,' my mother said, concentrating on the road. I looked sideways at her and noticed something I'd never really noticed before, that she didn't much like Archy. I asked myself why not, and I asked myself why I'd never really noticed before, and we lapsed a little into silence, looking at Vienna, which was beautiful at that time of year, or, indeed, as my mother would say, at any time of the year.

I looked forward through the car's windscreen, like a carsick child concentrating on his stomach. I looked forward at Vienna, rushing up to me and towering above me, the great big buildings. White and brown, filled with people, filled with people's love for them. They had evident and mysterious purposes, they were beautiful and ugly. They rushed up to the car, and then, my forward vision forgot them. They might have been scrunched up like paper and thrown away behind us, because I didn't look back. I felt as if I was recovering from a long, a day-long fit of weeping, as if I was exhausted and shaking and oddly satisfied, though really I was none of these things. My mother looked at me sideways in the car, and I could see she wanted to ask me about the strange look in my eye, and my morning with my grandmother, but she isn't the sort of person who can ask that kind of thing. Outside the opera house, so early, at three in the afternoon, my mother kissed me in a normal way, only her eyes giving out her concern. And then she said the same thing she had said an hour before, what she always said when I was a child, 'Be good.' And now I was grown up, I didn't do anything afterwards to let her down, to curdle the wish. I was good.

Sometimes you remember things when they happen, and sometimes you remember things as happening when they should have been important. When I think about my triumph now, I remember the moment of my grandmother's triumph as well. My grandmother rarely had these moments of glory we all worked towards. She often behaved as if she had nothing else, but now I think that this was the only one she ever had. Who was she proving herself against? Her father, her husband, Archy, me? What was she proving? I never found out, and I still don't know. I thought the story was complete, the story she told me in the art gallery. But I didn't know the rest of the story until later that night, until early the next morning. She told me as the light outside was going grey with the morning. But, maybe, as I began to sing, what I was singing about was not Berg's music, which had long ago left him and gone out into the world like an old streetwalker to pleasure thousands, but my grandfather's music, which no one knew, and my grandmother's final act of love, which only she knew.

I stood like a pillar, wrapped in gold silk as the curtain rose, and let myself be sung about. Berg died waiting for a performance which came too late; waiting, perhaps, for the performance I gave the night before my grandmother told me the story of her triumph. It perhaps wasn't a great performance, but it was the night which I think changed my life.

The *Lulu* began, full of death and longing and incompleteness. Like every performance I ever knew, it quickly went blank and automatic. The first act was so free of thought, so little laboured over that it surprised me when I had no more to sing, and I was standing over a prostrate baritone and sticking my chin out, and the curtain came down to a final spastic tumult in the orchestra. I was afraid for a moment that I had been standing there, not singing, not knowing what to do, quite blank, while the opera happened around me. But I knew nothing had gone wrong. I knew about my own gorgeousness.

I went back to the dressing room, and shut the door, just waiting for nothing. I thought about nothing then, but now, when I think about that half an hour, I think about Berg's death, which, after all, happened in the interval between two acts. It seemed always such a long walk from the dressing room to the stage. People who said always 'Good evening, Miss Weissmann,' whose names I never knew, got out of my way. I was deep in lack of thought. The second act began in the same way, with a vivid impression of the first seconds and then dullness as I rode over the long minutes without thought, just watching my voice overcoming problems. I moved about the stage like a figure on a clock.

Blankness comes and goes, and you can't always rely on it. And the only thing I can now remember about that performance was my blankness, which I had never asked for, but was always grateful for, abruptly fading. Before, I seemed to be floating, and doing only what I was told to do. But then, like a television screen warming, or a curtain dropping, everything was clear, and instead I was standing on a stage with terrifying clarity telling a man about himself in someone else's words, and in the audience, somewhere, was my grandmother, listening with pain to my voice. The Schön must have seen the panic on my face, because he turned his back on the audience and prepared to help me through it. We got through the argument somehow, through shouting a lot, and then he was kneeling on my neck and I knew exactly what to do, I was completely calm.

I threw the Schön from me and scrambled on to the table. From there it was no effort to leap to the chandelier, and the words came with a tremendous silent explosion, like a cold blaze of a mercury flare over the landscape of my fear.

'*Wenn sich die Menschen,*' I sang, to the end of the aria, swinging, seeing the audience almost agape, quite amazed, seeing the rest of the cast, who had seen me do it before, still importing a little real amazement into their stage amazement. The aria went off without trouble, and there was even a little spatter of applause over the baritone's re-entry. I dropped from the chandelier and gave myself a moment to recover. I had a gun, I didn't know where from, and the moment came to sing again, and I raised my head and sang.

'And that was all,' I sang. 'Nothing more. You then were gone, shooting your Doctor Schön (or am I Alwa? or Geschwitz, distanced by possibility and proximated by desire, as in her case by anatomy?) and not turning back. No jails exist, however, from which you need escape, no Geschwitzes who need contract scarlet fever, take your place. Your cry of *Freiheit* will be an interior one, a necessary avoidance of the melodrama no decent opera can do without.'

The baritone was staring at me, though he was supposed to be dead. The second conductor was waving his arms feebly from his shoe-box on stage, looking not at the score but, aghast, at me. Only then, seeing the unmoving cast around me, the unceasing catastrophes in the orchestra, did I realize what I had done, that I had begun to sing words not Lulu's, not Wedekind's, not Berg's, not even my grandmother's, but only Archy's. '*Was machst du denn für Unsinn?*' said the baritone's corpse as I knelt over it, a furious whisper. '*Scheiss macht frei,*' I said quietly to him. His eyes were away from the audience, and almost popping with rage.

Heinrich and the Schön were the only ones to worry about it, however. Heinrich knew where it came from, and the Schön thought I had gone mad. Everyone else in the cast assumed that I had forgotten the words and sung the first nonsense that came into my head, judiciously sprinkling a few names of characters in to make it sound authentic. I was happy to go along with this. It made things easier. As for the audience, I never heard that anyone realized that anything was wrong. Certainly no critic mentioned it, although more than one said that I might as well have been singing in Japanese.

I had a long time to recover between shooting Doctor Schön and coming out of prison, as it were, when everyone kept saying how well I had coped, how unlikely it was that anyone would have noticed a thing. I doubted it. After the second act there was a short break, and then the mime of the rest of the action, which was no effort and needed no concentration. I kept thinking about the third act, that other *Lulu*, in a safe in the house of a woman I had never met, a document I had never seen, and now probably never would see. Archy had told me that the widow of Berg was to come to the performance tonight. She was, I now saw, the most important listener to the opera, not just to the poor shards of the third act we'd managed to dig out. She had not been pointed out to me, and I was not to meet her. She had the third act, the real one, and she played no part whatever in my life, my Berg life.

Afterwards, when the congratulators and the fans and the flower-bearers had gone, and I looked in the mirror to clean off the fat stage make-up, there was a knock on the door. It was Archy, on his own.

'It's over,' he said.

'Everything?' I said. I carried on wiping, and he talked to my reflection.

'Everything,' he said. 'What else is there? Look, I brought a bottle of gin back. And, look, I remembered to bring glasses. I thought you might not have any.'

'I could have sent for some,' I said.

'Sorry,' he said.

'You haven't said that for so long,' I said. 'Sorry. Oh, I missed it. You're right. Nothing's real, is it?'

'Oh yes,' he said, pouring two glasses of gin. 'Plenty of things are real.'

'Don't worry,' I said. 'It'll do.' And, indeed, the things that were real would do. My grandfather really had been a good composer, and perhaps a great composer. What did my grandmother's pain matter, really? And the widow of Berg, who I had never met, really was his widow, and really had the rest of the opera. And that was enough.

'You were very good,' said Archy.

'What?' I said.

'You were very good,' he said again. 'Really wonderful.'

'Thank you,' I murmured. 'Nothing wrong?'

'No,' he said. 'Nothing wrong?'

'No,' I said. 'But I'm leaving you.'

'I thought so,' he said. 'I'm sorry. It was too late, wasn't it, for Berg. And for me, too. I think you ought to read this. Not now. Later.'

He handed me an envelope, thick with a letter. It had only my name on it, in Archy's confident hand. I wondered how far Archy had foreseen all this, and how far he had planned it all.

'Yes, all right,' I said. 'I'm sorry, too.'

'By the way,' he said, 'it's called a shooting stick. Your grandmother's stick.'

'What?'

'I told you once it was called a shoot stick. It's not. It's called a shooting stick.'

'Oh,' I said.

'I'm sorry,' he said. 'I thought it was funny at the time.'

'That's all right,' I said. 'It doesn't matter. Thanks for telling me. You know, I never did get to like gin.'

'No?' said Archy. 'Ah well.'

'I'm sorry about the words, tonight,' I said.

'That's all right,' he said. 'It was nothing. Really nothing. And what do the words matter, really, or who wrote them, or whether it's real, or really anything?'

'It's important to get things right,' I said, disconcerted.

'Yes,' said Archy. 'But everything was right. Everything is right.'

And he sat down in a chair, and silently watched me assemble my features from oil and butter, and prepare to face a little eager crowd, with their tiny black exploding boxes and their proffered chewed biros and their little books. I wanted, for once in my life, to make someone wait for me. And Archy, holding a grey hat which I had bought for him, and his old blue overcoat, sat and waited without talking.

THIRTY-SEVEN

I sat in my place, with Archy's letter in my bag, and I waited for them to speak to me.

'Marvellous,' said Archy.

'Really exceptional,' said Lady Harcourt, through Archy, later.

'Wonderfully well thought through,' said the Schön, later.

'Exquisite,' said Frau Egon, later.

'Quite remarkable,' said Lord Harcourt, later.

'Astounding,' said the Schön's wife, later.

'Incomparable,' said Heinrich, later.

'Beautiful,' said my mother, later.

'As good as I expected,' said Charlotte, heaving herself into her place, later. And some of them were talking about the food and some of them were talking about *Lulu*.

'My dear ladies,' said Lord Harcourt. 'As my son will no doubt have told you, I am something of an expert in these matters. Not professionally, I mean.'

'No, he has not,' said Frau Egon. 'I had really no idea that you were interested in stage design at all.'

'Not as such,' said Lord Harcourt. 'In modern painting, however.'

'Lord Harcourt,' I said, 'has a very important collection of modern abstract art.'

'Not all abstract,' said my grandmother. 'We have recently added to it.'

'What have you bought, Lady Harcourt?' said Archy.

Lady Harcourt interposed, thinking that she was being talked about and held up the conversation embarrassingly for a few minutes.

'What have you bought?' said Archy to my grandmother again.

'A second Betterave,' she said.

'Another mud picture?' I said.

'No,' she said.

'No,' said Lord Harcourt, 'a figurative painting. I wished it to be something which I, and perhaps my wife, could be associated with, so we approached Betterave directly. I do not believe in interfering with the creative process, of course. Artists must be free to produce whatever they wish to produce. But we both wished to draw out of Betterave something which he was interested in and which could, to posterity, be associated as much with us as with Betterave. I am not sure, either, that everything that Betterave has produced would please my dear wife so much in our house.'

'What is it?' said Archy.

'A portrait,' said my grandmother. 'Of the two of us. His style has quite changed, one would hardly know our two Betteraves are the same artist.'

'Ludwig and I have commissioned a portrait of him in costume,' said the Schön's wife. 'He had a great success in *Der Rosenkavalier* last season, as you recall, Frau Harcourt?'

'Yes,' I said. 'He was the baritone, wasn't he?'

The Schön's wife laughed heartily. 'Of course,' she said. 'What else?'

I flushed, at my own stupidity.

'But after that,' she went on, not minding, 'we wanted to have some kind of souvenir of it, as it were. So a friend of ours, a painter, you know, agreed very kindly to paint him in costume. It really looks very well, most imposing, most interesting. You were Sophie in the same production, weren't you?'

'Yes, I was,' I said. 'You do very well to remember the names of the characters. I never can.'

'It is a beautiful opera,' said Frau Egon. 'I remember the first time I saw it, and finding myself weeping at such beauty. I feel ashamed to say it, and I was most embarrassed that anyone saw me. The gentlemen who took me laughed at me for some time afterwards because I was so moved by it.'

'But why?' said the Schön's wife, genuinely perplexed. 'When Ludwig was in it last season, I went many times, and every time I and my friends wept. It is not a cause for embarrassment. Why feel shame?'

'I do not know,' said Frau Egon.

'I cry often,' said my grandmother; 'I enjoy it. I do not say that an evening is incomplete if one does not cry, of course.'

'You often do say that, my dear,' said Lord Harcourt.

'Yes, I do,' said my grandmother. 'But this evening, this *Lulu* was most beautiful and complete even without our weeping. You do not weep at it. It is complete without it, in a sense. I had the feeling that it had nothing to do with me.'

'Oh, you shouldn't feel that,' said Archy, as if he were only being polite.

'I don't understand,' said Heinrich. 'It's unfinished, isn't it? We all know that.'

'It is incomplete,' said my grandmother. 'In a sense it is. It needs another act. But even if there was a proper third act it would be complete only in the sense that it is complete now. And no more. I'm talking so badly.'

'Yes,' I said. 'I think I see. It's incomplete, but there's something about it that just says that it doesn't need anything else.'

'Yes,' my mother said. 'That's right. *Rosenkavalier* is too long, too polished, too everything really, but it's still unfinished. Do you see?'

'No,' said the Schön, raising his head at last from the plate. 'It's finished.'

'No,' said my mother. 'You don't see. Even when it's finished, it still needs someone to come along and say *Wie schön* to it, to weep and to join in with the big tune at the end. So on its own it's unfinished.'

'But what about *Lulu*?' I said to my grandmother. I had such strong hopes, just for a second, but I don't know what I was hoping for, exactly.

'When is your baby due?' said the Schön's wife to Charlotte.

'*Lulu* was quite a new experience for me, I must say,' said Lord Harcourt. 'As much as I love modern art, I cannot claim to be *au fait* with other modern art forms, and I seldom visit the opera unless it be for Mozart, whom I love. But I must say that *Lulu* was a great pleasure.'

'I'm sure,' said Charlotte brightly, wisely ignoring the Schön's wife, 'that it was a pleasure compounded by seeing Friederike in the leading role.'

'Indeed it was,' said Lord Harcourt, warming to his theme. 'A rare and unusual pleasure.'

Lady Harcourt suddenly smiled cheerily at me and said something in English to Archy.

'My mother's just said that she's having a very nice time,' said Archy.

'Tell her I'm glad,' I said, surprised.

'My son is a little inaccurate, I fear,' said Lord Harcourt. My – what she actually said was how delicious she finds your cooking and how kind it is of you to go to such lengths as to cook after such a strenuous performance.'

I beamed artificially at Lady Harcourt, who bowed back novelistically and began a conversation in English with Heinrich.

'What are your plans, Frau Harcourt?' the Schön said to me.

'None, I'm afraid,' I said, almost immediately understanding what he meant.

'We must find you something before Christmas, anyway,' he said.

'I don't know whether I could,' I said. 'I don't know whether I could face it.'

'Oh, why not?' said Heinrich, breaking off his conversation.

'I'm sure she has a very good reason,' said my grandmother, looking rather obviously at Charlotte. She often tried to suggest to people that I was pregnant, as if she could make me have a baby by suggesting it.

'No she doesn't,' said Archy. 'I'm sure she can do something if you've anything in mind.'

'It depends on her, really,' said the Schön, and both of them turned and looked at me. I looked back, a little hopelessly.

'There's really no point at all in bullying her in this way just after she's finished a performance,' my mother said. 'She must be exhausted, can't you see?'

'I'm not really,' I said. And it was true, that I seemed to have fed on everything this evening and drawn only strength from it all. 'I wish my grandfather could have seen it. I remember him so well. I remember the only time I ever heard him play his own music. I went round to sing there. Perhaps one time when you were there, Frau Egon. I was a little early and was waiting in the hall. My grandfather, you know, he often played the piano to himself when he thought no one was listening.'

'Oh, don't start on that,' said Archy. 'I've heard this story so many times.'

I looked at him in surprise.

'We should go,' said Heinrich. I did not know who he was including in his 'we' until I saw Lady Harcourt was gathering up her napkin and depositing it on the tablecloth. Archy was working hard at avoiding my gaze.

'But first,' said my grandmother, 'some music.'

'No, no,' said my mother. 'Friederike really shouldn't sing now.'

'Why not?' said my grandmother.

'It's three o'clock in the morning,' said my mother.

'I don't mind,' I said. 'I mean, I'd like to. But Archy has to choose the music.'

'That would be very pleasant,' said Lady Harcourt through her translators. Heinrich gave way with a bad grace, since he was obviously sleepy, and agreed to play the piano for me.

Archy, I saw, had assembled on the piano a *time-to-go-home* pile of music, and perhaps it was really his time to go home. I smiled at him, and in a way he smiled back. On the top of the pile was a Mozart aria and a Schubert ballad, both greeted with volleys of *Wie schön*ing. My mother excused herself, and Lord Harcourt offered to take her back to the hotel. Next, the last ten minutes of *Tristan und Isolde*, not ideal for confined spaces. At this point, a neighbour telephoned in a fit of rage, and Charlotte left in a taxi, refusing offers of lifts. Frau Egon, who was staying in the flat, went to bed. A piece of Schoenberg dispatched the Schön and his wife, offering Heinrich and Lady Harcourt a gratefully accepted lift. My grandmother sat alone in the middle of the empty chairs, and waited. Archy took over and we began the strategy in earnest. First, Charles Ives. My grandmother applauded. Secondly, a piece by Stockhausen. She bounced with pleasure. Thirdly, 'Martern aller Arten', sending its fusillades out into the grey beginnings of the Vienna dawn.

We reached the end and looked at her.

'Very fine,' she said. 'Very fine indeed. But now you are to come over here, and I shall talk to you seriously for a few minutes. I need to tell you the rest of the story.'

'Time-to-go-home, time-to-go-home,' Archy sang.

'Not for me,' she said. 'Come over here.'

Defeated, we went.

THIRTY-EIGHT

'I think there's something you ought to know,' said my grandmother. 'It's only one thing, but I have to tell Archy the whole story, before I tell you the last thing, the thing I didn't tell you this morning.' And then she told us everything. She told us the story of her glory. We were dropping with fatigue, barely able to listen or tell when she was saying something we didn't know already. And, now, when I look back on that immense evening and night and morning, I don't know if she was telling me something I didn't know already, or telling me something she hadn't told me in the morning, or if she was speaking at all.

She came to the end of her story.

'So it was ruined for you,' I said. 'All ruined.'

There was a long silence.

'And the manuscripts,' I said. 'Where are the manuscripts? Is that it?'

'I spoke to Mathilde about them,' she said.

She asked Mathilde to come with her, and together they went into the study where an entire shelf was piled high with the suave calligraphy and transparent beauty of his music. My grandmother passed Mathilde great sheafs of thick paper, and, weeping, Mathilde put it on the fire. Once she couldn't carry on. My grandmother stopped, and so that she didn't think she was being heartless, she said, 'It was just for us, you know, this music. And now it's just for me. And it always will be, because no one else will ever hear it. That's what he wanted.' For Mathilde, what my grandfather wanted was more important than anything, and she carried on, until everything was burnt, and in the grate a pile of incomparable ashes.

'You burnt everything?' I said.

'No,' she said. 'Not quite. There was one thing I couldn't burn. Here it is. Do what you want with it. It would have reminded me of Berg a week ago, so I couldn't listen to it. Now it would just remind me of what I have done. So I can't listen to it now, either.'

'How do you feel?' I said.

'I would do it again,' she said. 'He was wrong, he was so wrong. I did what I could to do the right thing. And I did.' I looked at her, expecting her familiar look of glory. And she looked at me, and there was something quite new in her look, and I didn't need to ask again.

'Don't wake your husband,' she said. 'It doesn't matter any more. It's all over. He didn't know what he was doing. And neither did you.'

Archy didn't know what he was doing, and neither did I, and neither did she. I wouldn't tell her the lies were Archy's, not Alban's. I kept my terrible knowledge, just for the moment. I picked up the one score left. It was a septet, and on the cover it said January 1970, which was the month before my grandfather died. And underneath, it said, For Friederike. It was the tender vulnerable remains of Archy's glory, and the surviving fragile witness of my grandmother's glory, and I turned to my husband, as my grandmother rose to leave the room, and I watched his forging hand fall over the edge of his chair in sleep, and I realized that that was all. Mine, but not Archy's, and not hers, but his, the beloved, his, always his.

I left the house, and I walked the streets of Vienna. I thought about my life, which stretched uneventfully in front of me like a plain of clouds beneath an aeroplane. I would be praised, and I would be attacked, and I would accept roles, and I would walk out of some productions, and I would be sacked from others, and I would sing in terrible performances of wonderful operas, and wonderful performances of terrible operas, and I would be paid; and virgins and cripples and bachelors and widows and the happy and the unhappy and children and homosexuals and dwarves and giants and invalids and Australians would pin my photograph to walls, and they were walls I would never see. And nothing would go wrong with my life, and the chance of glory might come before me, and there would, after all that, be a happy ending.

I thought about my grandmother, with her title, and her beast for a husband, and her misery, and I thought that, just like one of the heroines in Archy's tripy paperbacks, I had won over her, and I wondered how, and why. I thought about Archy, and his letter, which, once I found a café which was open, I would read. I thought about my mother. And I thought about my grandfather, and his septet.

The cafés didn't open early in Vienna, unless they had customers who were up then. So I found one near the flower market, where I could sit and read, where soft blossoms are unloaded like cabbages, and lives begin before the sun rises.

> Dear Luise, dear Friederike. Perhaps this is the moment to drop another's voice, to speak in my own voice. But perhaps not. Perhaps it is better, after all, to return to the time when I almost made a success of things, almost transformed my life, and almost found myself at the centre of my own life. Ironic, then, that I only achieved it by taking on the voice, the sound, the verbal gait of another.
>
> But I shall not write about him, that great dead master whom I love better than anyone; who has not loved me well in return. This letter is to you, my wife; and, although this could, and should, be Berg speaking, it is not about Berg. Rather, the difficulty of what I must say requires me to

return to a moment, and a style, when I knew how to speak, and knew how to write. Because, now, I wish and need to speak of love, and the loss of love, and the need for love.

Never did I speak readily of love; of my love for you, of your love for me. Was it necessary? Did you feel a shy, impossible to fulfil, impossible to postpone, desire to tell me of your love for me? I never knew it, if you did; I never did it, if you knew. And now, it is too late, and perhaps only in a letter, perhaps only even in a letter left to be read after my death, could I ever have said such a thing. But I begin to think of writing of love, and my pen turns to granite in my hand. It is too late, it was ever too late.

An ordinary heroine would need now to ask a question which, though asked of the past, is weighed down by the present so as never to receive any answer. They would ask, as I am not going to ask, 'What went wrong?' Though I say I shall not ask, writing it makes me ponder. Perhaps when I stopped being able to teach you, stopped being able to tell you your faults, perhaps it was then; perhaps it was when you slept with my father (Oh, I knew, I knew; do not think I am ever unaware of anything, as you always have until now). I have been faithful to you, as you have been unfaithful to me. But I shall not envisage causes which are about to lead me to tell you that I shall divorce you, though I find that some have written themselves down. It is too late for that, and perhaps it has ever been too late.

I do not know where I shall go, but I know well where you are to go. You know it well too, now, and I am the last person in the world who can tell you a thing you know so well, which fills you with such presentiment, such joy, such future. You are filled with my future, and I leave you. You see, like those thick books I like, we find we are having a happy ending. The villain is despatched to live out his life in exile. The wicked witch is in a hell of her own making. And the heroine, against all odds, has achieved what she wanted, and lives happily ever after. How like *Lulu*. But remember, even *Lulu* has a third act, although I do not expect you recall what happens in it. And now, finally, though you do not need me to say it, *Leb wohl. Leb wohl. Leb wohl.*

Your Archy. Your Alban.

I took the letter, in Archy's hand, and in his own voice, and folded it and put it in my bag. I left the café, full of people who had no idea who I was, when it was time to go. I walked out, and looked up to the sky, and waited for the light to fall on me, gathering my coat around me in the early morning cold. And I think then I turned round, and began the long unshepherded walk home, the ache at the back of my calves like thunder in summer, as the people of the city began to leave their houses and live their right-way-up lives.

THIRTY-NINE

That was all, really. When I got home, I went to bed and slept for twenty-two hours. I woke up at seven in the morning the morning after, and the others were all gathered round my bed with grave faces, as if they were waiting for me to die.

Everything, and nothing, seemed to have changed. I told Archy there was no point in our getting a divorce, and he agreed. I took his worked-over, inaccurate, absurd letter, and destroyed it. There was no particular reason for changing my mind, but I was sure I was doing the right thing. Nothing had changed, after all. Archy was still the Archy I had married, and even if that was my fault, it was too late to do anything about it. It was too late for him to do anything about it.

My grandmother stayed on for a few more days with my mother, after Lord Harcourt had gone. She seemed diminished, older, frailer, and my mother scolded her for exhausting herself.

'But it was worth it. After all,' said my grandmother, 'isn't Vienna the most beautiful of cities at this time of year?'

'Or,' said my mother, 'at any time of year?'

During those few days, we were like ordinary people. I cooked for my husband. Archy stayed in the flat and read paperback novels. My mother assumed he read them because he found them absurd and politely asked him to read her any especially silly bits. Archy, however, read them because he liked them, and just went on reading. They went back to Berlin together, my mother and grandmother, to oversee the packing-up of her furniture and the sacking of Mathilde before my grandmother went back to England. I had seen a previous attempt to sack Mathilde, which had quickly changed into an attempt – eventually successful – to persuade Mathilde not to walk out on them. I didn't envy them the task.

The task remained of putting Archy right about the affair he thought I had had with his father, and I went to the market to practise the conversation I was going to have with him. There was no food worth buying, and in the end I went for a walk and came home again empty-handed.

No one answered the door when I rang the bell, and I let myself in. 'Archy,' I called from the hall. There was no reply, but there were voices in the drawing room, and I went in.

'But after all,' Charlotte was saying, 'after all that.'

They often practised piano duets together, Archy and Charlotte, like two English virgins in the morning. Seeing that I had come in, they turned to the piano and began to play. I sat down and listened for a bit. They sat together on one long piano stool, the one I bought after I'd destroyed the old one to get at a manuscript. Archy's fidgety wriggle as he played, Charlotte's stately bowing over her fecundity, in time to the music. Her careful, pregnant accuracy, his plunks and approximations.

From the way they sat, and from the way they didn't need to look at each other while they played, I knew that one day, perhaps soon, or perhaps not soon at all, I would come into a room, just in this way, and find Archy licking the long white inner arm of Charlotte. Or holding her hair from her face. Or with his hands to her throat. But it didn't matter. I saw it with such clarity, the scene, and Charlotte looking at me with enormous scared eyes. The eyes of a child, with a child inside her. For a moment I was shocked, and then I was shocked that I wasn't more shocked. I was actually only pleased that Archy had someone to teach all over again, and I liked the way she looked at me with respect, as if I had won a game and couldn't be argued with.

When she went, I said, 'Archy.'

'Yes,' he said.

'That was lovely,' I said. 'I think your piano playing is improving.'

'Thank you,' he said.

'You know the letter you wrote me?'

'Yes,' he said.

And then my nerve failed, and all I said was 'Did you keep a copy of it?'

'No,' he said, looking at me strangely. 'Of course not. Did you keep it?'

'No,' I said. 'Of course not.'

'Well then,' he said, turning round and beginning to play Dvořák again, actually rather badly. So I never did get to tell him. Much later, Charlotte asked Archy to be her daughter's godfather. When we call at her cold flat with some baby clothes, or, later, an enormous bear, or, later, a party dress, or, later, a string of pearls for her confirmation, or, later still, later still, diamonds for her wedding, her fatherless girl looks at us over the banisters as if we were as happy as the presents made her. And at first, she looked at us, without happiness or misery, just accepting. But later, she smiled, and now, when I call at her Vienna house, when I am in Vienna, she says, just like Mathilde once did, 'Neither one nor the other of you ever warn me when you're coming, do you?' She says it in her sweet, slow voice, which she only ever uses for speaking. And then, unlike Mathilde, she smiles, as if she knew what Archy was like; as if she were the only one of us who ever knew what Archy was capable of, and always knew what Archy could never ever do, knew it before she was born. She's the person, who, if I enlisted anyone, I should enlist to tell Archy that I never had an affair with his father, but somehow I never manage to ask her. And perhaps it doesn't matter any more. She looks at me with sweetness and fondness, and there are always other things to talk about.